The intensity of his stare made her remember the dream she'd been trying all day to forget...

The two of them had been—

No!

She couldn't allow herself to have *those* thoughts about Nathan.

He looked down at her, and in the soft light his eyes were like obsidian pools—deep and fathomless. Dangerous, if you weren't careful.

He reached out a hand to touch her hair.

"Don't do something we'll both regret," she warned. But she didn't move away from his touch.

"I would never ask you to do anything you didn't really want to." Nathan wove his fingers in her hair, applying a gentle pressure until they stood only inches apart. He was so tall, she had to look up at him, and when she tilted her head back, he lowered his mouth to hers.

Her first thought was to shove him away. Let him know she was not his for the taking.

Instead, she stood perfectly still, allowing his lips to whisper over hers in a promise of passion....

Dear Harlequin Intrigue Reader,

We have another outstanding title selection this month chock-full of great romantic suspense, starting with the next installment in our TOP SECRET BABIES promotion. In *The Hunt for Hawke's Daughter* (#605) by Jean Barrett, Devlin Hawke had never expected to see Karen Ramey once she'd left his bed—let alone have her tell him his secret child had been kidnapped by a madman. Whether a blessing or a curse, Devlin was dead set on reclaiming his child—and his woman....

To further turn up the heat, three of your favorite authors take you down to the steamy bayou with *three* of the sexiest bad boys you'll ever meet: Tyler, Nick and Jules—in *one value-packed volume!* A bond of blood tied them to each other since youth, but as men, their boyhood vow is tested. Find out all about *Bayou Blood Brothers* (#606) with Ruth Glick—writing as Rebecca York—Metsy Hingle and Joanna Wayne.

Amanda Stevens concludes our ON THE EDGE promotion with *Nighttime Guardian* (#607), a chilling tale of mystery and monsters set in the simmering South. To round out the month, Sheryl Lynn launches a new series with *To Protect Their Child* (#608). Welcome to McCLINTOCK COUNTRY, a Rocky Mountain town where everyone has a secret and love is for keeps.

More action and excitement you'll be hard-pressed to find. So pick up all four books and keep the midnight oil burning....

Sincerely,

Denise O'Sullivan
Associate Senior Editor
Harlequin Intrigue

NIGHTTIME GUARDIAN
AMANDA STEVENS

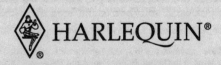

TORONTO • NEW YORK • LONDON
AMSTERDAM • PARIS • SYDNEY • HAMBURG
STOCKHOLM • ATHENS • TOKYO • MILAN • MADRID
PRAGUE • WARSAW • BUDAPEST • AUCKLAND

Many thanks to Phyllis Holmes, manager of Pearls Unique in Newport, Arkansas. Without her invaluable assistance, this book would never have been written.

Please forgive any mistakes I made about the pearling industry. I tried to do it justice.

ISBN 0-373-22607-1

NIGHTTIME GUARDIAN

Copyright © 2001 by Marilyn Medlock Amann

Visit us at www.eHarlequin.com

Printed in U.S.A.

ABOUT THE AUTHOR

Amanda Stevens has written over twenty novels of romantic suspense. Her books have appeared on several bestseller lists, and she has won Reviewer's Choice and Career Achievement in Romantic/ Mystery awards from *Romantic Times Magazine*. She resides in Cypress, Texas, with her husband, her son and daughter and their two cats.

Books by Amanda Stevens

Don't miss any of our special offers. Write to us at the following address for information on our newest releases.

Harlequin Reader Service
U.S.: 3010 Walden Ave., P.O. Box 1325, Buffalo, NY 14269
Canadian: P.O. Box 609, Fort Erie, Ont. L2A 5X3

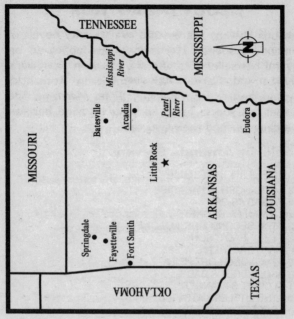

All underlined places are fictitious.

CAST OF CHARACTERS

Shelby August—Twenty-one years ago she saw something rise out of the river and come after her. Whether the monster was real or imagined, Shelby's life has never been the same since that night.

Nathan Dallas—For over two decades he's kept his feelings for Shelby a secret. Now she's come back home, but another terrible secret threatens to keep them apart.

Annabel Westmoreland—Shelby's grandmother has lived on the river most of her life. She's seen a lot of strange things.

Yoshi Takamura—He's built a laboratory near the river, and there are whispers in town of strange experiments.

James Westmoreland—Annabel's son. How far would he go to get his hands on her money?

Delfina Boudreaux—Her midnight walks along the river are troubling. What is she looking for?

Virgil Dallas—After Shelby's monster sighting, his paper made the nine-year-old famous…and then infamous.

Miss Scarlett—Annabel's neurotic cat may be the death of Shelby yet.

Dear Reader,

They say you can't go home again, but *Nighttime Guardian* took me straight back to my roots along the White River in Arkansas. The journey started, oddly enough, on the Internet when I came across a site for a jewelry store in Newport, Arkansas, which deals in freshwater pearls from the White and Black Rivers. I was fascinated to learn that river pearls can be worth thousands of dollars and that in the late 1800s a White River pearl was mounted in the royal crown of England!

I was hooked. Intrigued. But I still didn't quite have the spark I needed for my story. Then one day Phyllis Holmes, the manager of the store, reminded me about the White River Monster. That prehistoric, sea-serpent-like creature, affectionately dubbed Ole Whitey by the locals, had been the stuff of local legends. I began to wonder what would happen to a child who had a close encounter with the monster. How would she function in a world that didn't believe in such creatures?

In *Nighttime Guardian* I've changed the name of the river and created a fictitious town, populated with fictitious characters. I've even taken artistic license with the monster. But make no mistake. This is where I grew up. These are my people.

And the monster? Well, a 1973 resolution was passed in the Arkansas state legislature creating the White River Monster Refuge.

Now, to you city folk, this may seem a mite eccentric. But if you're ever out on the river at midnight, when the air is still and the shadows deep and the water so murky it's like pea soup, you won't think it strange. Not one bit.

Amanda Stevens

Prologue

From the *Arcadia Argus,* June 18, 1980:

Pearl River Monster Strikes Again!
Well, folks, just when you thought it was safe
to go back in the water, the Pearl River Monster
has reared its ugly head again. A few days ago,
a couple of local farmers reported missing livestock, and another one says he found a mutilated
cow carcass down by the river. Now little
Shelby Westmoreland, Annabel Westmoreland'sgranddaughter, has told Sheriff McCaid
that she saw a huge scaly beast rise up out of
the river last night right around midnight.

Unlike previous eyewitness accounts, which
claimed the Pearl River Monster resembled
some sort of prehistoric sea serpent, this creature apparently walked upright, like a man.

The child was clearly terrified and what she
described ''sent cold chills down my spine,''
said McCaid.

Just what little Shelby was doing out there
alone at that time of night is still unclear, but

one thing seems certain, folks. There is something in that river besides pearls and catfish....

From the *Arkansas Democrat,* June 25, 1980:

Nine-Year-Old Sees Monster

An Arcadia girl swears she saw a "huge scaly monster" rise out of the water near her grandmother's home on the Pearl River. The nine-year-old's claim is the most recent in a rash of Pearl River Monster sightings that have swept the small communities along the river in the wake of reports of missing livestock and cattle mutilations. Cross County Sheriff Roy McCaid told a group of reporters outside the courthouse yesterday that the child either saw something that badly frightened her, or else she's a very accomplished actress. "I've never seen a kid that scared. She could hardly talk when her grandmother brought her in."

The child's grandmother, Annabel Westmoreland, who deals in freshwater pearls harvested from the river, says her granddaughter left their house just before midnight on a dare from one of her friends. According to the grandmother, the child came running back to the house, screaming that she'd seen a horrible creature rise out of the water and come after her.

From the *Wall Street Journal,* July 2, 1980:

Monster Hunters Invade Arkansas

Following a recent Pearl River Monster sighting

by a nine-year-old girl, an army of scientists, sightseers and so-called monster hunters have descended on the small, northeast Arkansas town of Arcadia, located on the Pearl River.

In addition to missing and mutilated livestock—supposedly the handiwork of the monster—there have been numerous alleged sightings of a "huge, scaly, humanoid creature" that inhabits the river.

In Arcadia, where Shelby Westmoreland lives with her grandmother, feelings are mixed concerning the sightings. "We're all spooked around here," one woman says uneasily.

But another resident openly scoffs at the notion of a monster. "That girl is obviously trying to get herself some attention." The woman admits, however, that she has started locking her doors at night and might have second thoughts about swimming in the river.

Meanwhile, nine-year-old Shelby has become something of a celebrity, with tabloid reporters camping on her doorstep and an appearance scheduled later this week on the "Tonight" show.

From the *Arkansas Democrat,* July 9, 1980:

The Vanishing Monster

Three weeks after the latest and most dramatic sighting of the Pearl River Monster, scientists from Arkansas State University and from the Arkansas Game and Fish Commission have pulled up stakes and gone home. "If there is something living in that river other than an assortment of freshwater fish and mollusks, it certainly knows how to camouflage itself," says Dr. Dean Carey, a zoology professor in Jonesboro. "We've found no evidence of anything out of the ordinary in the Pearl River, except, unfortunately, for a high level of pollution."

Dr. Carey speculates that what people along the river may have witnessed recently is an alligator gar, which can sometimes reach lengths of ten to twelve feet. "And they aren't your most attractive creatures," he adds. "I can see how a child might think it a monster, particularly at night."

When asked how an alligator gar might "rise up out of the river," he laughs. "Chalk it up to a child's vivid imagination. That's the only possible explanation."

From the *Arcadia Argus,* July 16, 1980:

Monster Sighting A Clever Hoax?
Well, it looks like we've all been had, but it was a fun ride while it lasted. Sheriff McCaid now believes Shelby Westmoreland's claim that she saw the Pearl River Monster a month ago was, in fact, a hoax perpetrated by the girl's uncle, James Westmoreland, to capitalize on the influx of sightseers to the area.

According to the sheriff, business at the Pearl Cove probably increased by as much as tenfold during the weeks following little Shelby's claim. Anxious for a souvenir, visitors to the jewelry store were willing to plunk down hundreds of dollars for freshwater pearls from the river, guaranteed to protect the wearer from the monster.

With her uncle's confession, Shelby's fifteen minutes of fame have officially come to an end. Following recent developments, her second scheduled appearance on the "Tonight" show has been canceled, and the tabloid reporters have all gone home. Evidently, their feelings now are that the girl's story just isn't very credible.

Let's hope little Shelby doesn't go crying wolf in the near future because it's doubtful anyone would be willing to listen....

Chapter One

Twenty-one years later...

Nathan Dallas swatted a mosquito on the back of his neck as he guided the Buford boys' aluminum fishing skiff across the dusky water. The two brothers sat in the prow, drinking and muttering to one another until Nathan couldn't help but wonder what they might be up to. He'd been gone from Arcadia for a lot of years, but he still remembered the rumors that had always swirled around the Bufords.

He remembered a lot of other things, too. The river stirred powerful memories for him. His father, strong and agile, diving into those murky depths for pearls. His mother, gentle and pensive, calling Nathan in to supper.

And Shelby, suntanned and sweet, waiting for him on the bank.

Cutting the outboard motor, he let the boat drift. In the ensuing silence, the twilight came strangely alive. A few feet from the skiff, a water moccasin glided like a ribbon of silk toward the bank. Somewhere nearby a turtle plopped into the water, and a whippoorwill called from the branches of a sweet gum.

The melancholy sound brought back even more memories. The nights Nathan had camped out alone by the river because he couldn't stand seeing the grief in his father's face, the defeat that had stooped Caleb Dallas's shoulders and dulled his eyes before he'd reached fifty.

Back then Nathan had sworn he would never be caught in the same trap that had drained the youth from his father. He'd get away from this river if it was the last thing he did. He'd make something of his life, be somebody. And no one—especially not a woman—would ever take it away from him.

Well, at least that part had come true. His downfall hadn't been caused by a woman. It had been his own hubris that had wiped out his career and his good name. And now here he was, back where he'd started. Back on the river, but this time, he wasn't diving for mussel shells with his father. Caleb Dallas was dead, and Nathan now hunted something far more precious than pearls. A story that could launch his comeback. An exposé that could not only restore his reputation, but the self-respect he'd so carelessly tossed away in Washington.

He let his gaze travel downstream to where spotlights illuminated Takamura Industries. Yoshi Takamura had made millions selling freshwater mollusk shells to the Japanese cultured-pearl industry, but now that the mussel beds in the Pearl River were badly depleted, he'd turned his attention elsewhere.

He'd built a laboratory along the water, but to what end no one in town seemed to know. Or care, for that matter. Takamura was too important to the local economy for anyone to get overly concerned about their activities. But the secretive nature of the lab had triggered Nathan's natural curiosity.

He'd cultivated a deep throat on the inside, a man named Danny Weathers who was an old school buddy of Nathan's and who now worked as a diver for Takamura. So far, Danny hadn't been able to shed much light on the activities inside the lab, but Nathan wasn't about to give up. Not when he smelled a story.

At the other end of the boat, Ray Buford slapped at his bare leg. ''Hellfire, Bobby Joe. Why'd you go and forget the bug spray? Skeeters gonna eat us alive out here.''

''Not if you get enough alcohol in your bloodstream. This is better'n any old bug spray.'' Bobby Joe drained the last of his beer, smashed the empty can against his forehead, then slung the can overboard with a bloodcurdling yell.

Frowning, Nathan watched the container sink. Obviously, the Bufords didn't put much stock in river conservation. No wonder the Pearl River suffered from such dangerous levels of pollution. Nathan was sorely tempted to give them both a stern lecture, but he doubted it would do any good, and besides, he didn't want to risk alienating them. They both worked part-time for Takamura, and Nathan figured if the brothers got drunk enough, they might be willing to talk to him—which was precisely the reason he'd convinced them to let him help run their fishing lines tonight.

"Hey, wouldn't it be funny if we saw that ol' monster out here tonight?" Bobby Joe drawled.

"Yeah," Ray replied dryly. "That'd be real hilarious, Bobby Joe."

The younger Buford laughed, belched then pulled a wicked-looking knife from his belt and trailed it in the water. "Here monster, monster, monster. Where are you, boy? Come show that ugly face of yours. Make us famous."

"What're you, stupid or something?" Ray grumbled. "Shut the hell up."

"Chill, man." Bobby Joe made a chopping motion in the water with the switchblade. "That monster comes up here, I'll show him, like I did ol' Shorty Barnes that time."

Shorty Barnes was the reason Bobby Joe had spent three years in Cummins Prison Farm, but Nathan wasn't about to remind him of that fact.

"You'd show him all right," Ray scoffed. "Hell, boy. He'd chomp your arm off in one bite, knife and all."

"Sounds like you boys believe all those stories about the Pearl River Monster," Nathan said.

"Oh, Ray believes all right. He saw that thing himself, didn't you, bro?" There was a goading quality in Bobby Joe's thick voice. "Go ahead, tell 'im."

Ray didn't say anything, but in the fading light, Nathan saw something that might have been fear flicker across his homely features.

Unlike Bobby Joe, Nathan wasn't about to ridicule Ray Buford for his fears. Nathan used to dive in this river, in water so murky he sometimes couldn't see his hand in front of his face. There'd been times when he'd become so disoriented, he couldn't tell up from down, and in a cold, black panic, he'd sensed things he'd never told anyone about.

Twenty-one years ago, he'd never been as certain as everyone else in this town that Shelby Westmoreland had been lying.

An uneasiness settled over the boat. They were in the middle of the river now, over the deepest part. The water was more than fifty feet in places. Nathan had often wondered what kind of creatures could survive on that cold, muddy bottom. Man-sized catfish, if legend could be believed.

But it was the giant river loggerheads that had always given Nathan a healthy dose of caution. Diving in water populated by those creatures wasn't for the faint of heart. Also known as alligator snapping turtles, they sometimes grew to over two hundred pounds, and Nathan had once seen a smaller one snap a broom handle in two with its powerful jaws. He hated to think what one of the larger specimens could do to a man's hand.

The boat drifted toward the first marker, and Ray reached over the side of the boat to grab the white bleach jug fastened to the end of the trotline. He gave it a yank. "Damn. The line's tangled."

"Looks like one of us'll have to go down and get it freed up." Bobby Joe fingered his knife. They both looked at Nathan.

He reached over the side of the boat and grabbed the line. "Let's try working it loose first."

They tugged and pulled for several minutes before the line finally snapped free. Bobby Joe grunted as they hauled it up. "Musta hooked us a big sucker."

When the line popped to the surface, Ray leaned over the side to get a look. "What the hell is that?"

The realization hit all three of them at once, and Ray yelped, jerking back so violently the boat threatened to tip. Nathan clung to the sides as he stared at the mass of flesh and bone tangled in the line.

"Man, oh, man," Bobby Joe said almost reverently. "Would you look at that? Something's done ripped that poor bastard all to hell."

Ray didn't say anything. He stared at the corpse with a look of sheer terror, flinching almost pitifully when the beam of Nathan's flashlight accidentally caught him in the face.

Nathan leaned over the edge of the boat, playing the light over the body, what was left of it. The black neoprene wet suit was in shreds, but the mask was still in place. Sightless eyes stared up through the lens, and an icy chill sliced through Nathan.

The dead man was Danny Weathers.

Chapter Two

Exhaustion tightened the muscles in Shelby August's neck and shoulders, and she lifted her hand from the steering wheel to massage the soreness. Not so much exhaustion as tension, she realized, feeling the knots. Ever since she'd left the hospital in Little Rock where her grandmother had been admitted two days ago, Shelby had been experiencing a strange sense of disquiet, an uneasiness that had strengthened the farther north she drove on the interstate.

An hour out of Little Rock, she took the Arcadia exit, bypassing downtown to head east on a paved road that would take her to the river. A few miles in the opposite direction would have put her in the foothills of the majestic Ozarks, but Shelby came from the river bottoms—acres and aces of flat, swampy farmland steeped in superstition and mosquitoes.

Trees rose on either side of the road, obliterating the sky in places and turning the countryside almost pitch-black. The farther from town she drove, the more primal her surroundings. If she rolled down her window, she would be able to smell the river. But Shelby kept her windows up and her doors locked.

"Coward," she muttered. She was thirty years old, no longer the same little girl who had cried "monster" more than two decades ago. But if the passing years had dimmed her memory of that night, time had done nothing to convince her that monsters didn't exist. She knew all too well that they did.

But real monsters didn't creep up from the river in the dead of night, as she'd once believed. They walked into offices in broad daylight and killed for the contents of a safe.

He can't hurt you now, Shelby. You know that, don't you?

She could picture Dr. Minger sitting behind his desk, his kind eyes soft and a bit blurred by the thick lenses in his glasses. *Albert Lunt is in prison, serving a life sentence. No chance for parole. It's over.*

But it wasn't over, Shelby thought, fingering the silk scarf she wore at her throat. It never would be.

Months of therapy had helped. The nightmares were fewer and farther between now, but they still came. Albert Lunt still terrorized Shelby's sleep just as surely as he'd done the day he'd murdered her husband. Or the night he'd broken into her home and tried to kill her. As long as he was alive, he would always have this terrible hold on her.

I'll find a way to get you, he'd promised as the police had dragged him from her home that night.

And a part of Shelby still believed—would always believe—that he would.

She shivered, even though the evening was warm and humid and the air conditioner in her rental car was turned low. She reached over and shut off the fan, wishing she could turn off her memories as easily. But they were there, niggling at the fringes of her mind as they had been ever since she'd left L.A. Distance wouldn't quiet them, nor time. Nothing would.

Outside, the night deepened. Through the patches of trees, she had an occasional glimpse of moonlight on water. A silvery ribbon that wound for miles and miles through the very heart of Arkansas, the Pearl River had once held a fascination for Shelby, and then terror, after that summer. Now she realized that she had been hoping it might hold the key to her salvation.

Sixteen months, she thought numbly, as her head-lights picked out the last curve in the road before she reached her grandmother's house. Michael had been gone for over a year. Sometimes it seemed like only a heartbeat ago that the two of them had been planning their future together. Sometimes it seemed like a lifetime. Those times were the hardest, when Shelby would lie awake at night, unable to remember what he'd looked like. Oh, she could recall his beautiful grey eyes, the sound of his voice, the way he smiled. But she had trouble putting all those features together, making him seem real again.

It's time to let go, Shelby.

I can't. It's my fault he's dead. If I hadn't been late—

Lunt would have killed you, too. You know that.

Getting out of L.A. was a good idea, Dr. Minger had said. There were too many memories that bound her to the tragedy. She'd been trapped in a terrible limbo since Michael's death, not seeing friends, not going to work. Their savings and the proceeds from the sale of Michael's business had enabled her to let her career as an accountant slide into obscurity because she hadn't wanted to cope with the day-to-day pressures of getting on with her life.

If it hadn't been for her grandmother's call for help, Shelby wasn't certain she would have yet had the courage to break free.

Around the curve, the silhouette of her grandmother's house, perched on wooden stilts, came into view, but the sight of flashing lights down by the river almost stopped Shelby's heart. For one terrible moment, she thought she was back in L.A., back in her husband's office, bending over his lifeless body while the sirens wailed outside.

Then she thought of her grandmother, but Shelby quickly reminded herself that she'd left Annabel little more than an hour ago. Her grandmother was safe in the hospital and slowly on the mend. This had nothing to do with her.

Her uncle James? No. James didn't like the river. He had a place in town now. This was nothing to do with him, either.

But the reassurances didn't stop Shelby's hands from trembling as she pulled into her grandmother's drive, parked the car and got out. The lawn ran to the edge of an incline that dropped gently to the river. Several police cars and a hearse were parked along the road, and she could hear voices down by the water. With increasing trepidation, she walked across the yard and stood at the top of the bank, gazing down. A flashlight caught her in its beam, and someone shouted up to her. After a moment, a policeman scurried up the slope toward her.

"Get back in your car, Miss, and move along. This is police business."

"But I live here." She waved her hand toward the house.

"Annabel Westmoreland owns this place, ma'am. I happen to know she's in the hospital."

"I'm her granddaughter," Shelby said a bit defensively. "I'm going to be staying here for a while."

The deputy cocked his head. "Shelby?" He shone the flashlight in her face, and she flinched. "Sorry." He doused the light. "You are Shelby, aren't you?"

"Yes." She still didn't know who he was.

He chuckled ruefully. "Guess you don't recognize me in the uniform. No one ever expected a Millsap to be on this side of the law."

"Millsap?" she said incredulously. "Dewayne?"

He nodded and grinned. "Been with the county sheriff's department almost ten years now."

The Millsaps, along with their cousins, the Bufords, had once terrorized all of Cross County and half of Graves County. No one had ever expected any of them to amount to a hill of beans, as her grandmother would say.

"What happened, Dewayne?" Shelby asked uneasily. "Why are the police here?"

His expression sobered. "My cousins found a body tangled in one of their trot lines."

Shelby caught her breath. "Oh, no. Who was it?"

He hesitated, then shrugged. "Guess it won't matter if I tell you, seeing as how we've already notified his next of kin. His name was Danny Weathers. He was a local diver."

"How did he...die?"

"Looks like a boating accident. The coroner's down there now." Dewayne nodded toward her grandmother's house. "Look, maybe you best go on inside. This isn't something you want to see."

"But—"

"Hey, Dewayne!"

He turned at the sound of his name, then muttered a curse as a tall figure topped the bank and headed across the yard toward them. "Pardon my French, but I sure as hell don't need this tonight," he muttered to Shelby. He called to the newcomer, "Look, you got questions, you need to talk to the sheriff, Nathan."

Shelby's mouth fell open in astonishment. Nathan? Nathan Dallas? The boy who had once gotten her into so much trouble? Was it possible?

She'd heard Nathan had left this part of the country years ago. Like her, he'd migrated to a big city. Her grandmother had told her once that he was some hotshot reporter in Washington, just as he'd always said he would be. What in the world was he doing back in Arcadia?

"McCaid won't talk to me, you know that. Come on, Dewayne, cut me some slack here, okay?" Nathan strode over to the deputy, his back to Shelby. "I want to know what the coroner found when he examined the body."

Dewayne sighed. "And have my words splashed across the *Argus*? No thanks. Been there, done that."

"You got burned once by my uncle," Nathan said. "But you're dealing with me now. If you say something is off the record, it's off the record."

"Yeah, right."

Nathan ignored the sarcasm. "You don't really think this was a boating accident, do you? Come on."

"What else would cut a man up like that?" Dewayne said grimly. "He got caught in a boat propeller."

...cut a man up?

Shelby shivered uncontrollably. She'd forgotten how dangerous the river could be, how unpredictable. She'd come here seeking solace from the violence of her past only to find more death, more horror. But surely this was an accident. A terrible, tragic mishap.

"It's how he got caught in a prop that makes me curious," Nathan persisted. "Why was he out there diving alone?"

"His wife said he liked to go night-diving."

"Night-diving? In that river?" Nathan's tone was clearly incredulous.

Dewayne shrugged. "He got too close to the surface and a boat ran him over. Probably thought they hit a log or something."

"So that's going to be the party line, is it?" Contempt crept into Nathan's voice. "Are you even going to question Takamura?"

"That's none of your damn business," Dewayne countered. "You let the police handle the investigation."

"Which means you're not." Nathan shook his head in disgust. "Takamura's got an iron clamp on this town's throat, that's for damn sure."

The deputy's voice hardened with anger. "I don't think I like what you're implying, Nathan."

"No," Nathan said quietly. "I don't imagine you do."

Shelby had stood silently during this exchange, but Dewayne glanced at her now. "Look, I don't have time for this. I have to get back down there. It was nice seeing you again, Shelby."

"You, too, Dewayne."

Nathan spun, peering at her in the moonlight. As Dewayne walked away, Nathan took a few steps toward her. "Did I hear him right? Shelby? Shelby Westmoreland?"

"It's August now. It's been a long time, Nathan."

"At least you remember me," he said.

"Oh, I remember you all right." She wasn't likely to forget the kid who had dared her to meet him down by the river at midnight so they could watch for the Pearl River Monster together. Nor would she forget that he'd stood her up that night. If he'd been there to corroborate her story, Shelby never would have become such an object of ridicule.

At least that was the way she'd felt back then. But time had put that night in perspective. It hadn't been Nathan's fault that her imagination had conjured up a monster, or that, after the initial terror, she'd enjoyed the rush of attention. It hadn't been his fault that maybe, just maybe, she'd embellished her memory of that night because the spotlight had somehow made her abandonment more bearable. She'd been dropped on her grandmother's doorstep that summer by parents who didn't want her. Didn't love her. But for a while, everyone in Arcadia had adored her.

Then, of course, they'd turned on her.

But Nathan hadn't. He'd broken his word to her

that night, but he'd stood by her in the humiliating days afterward.

Hey, Shelby, seen any monsters lately?

Where's your monster, Shelby?

You shut your face, Nathan would tell the smirking crowd of kids who gathered around Shelby. *Before I shut it for you.*

And then, inevitably, a fight would ensue. Nathan had been so scrawny, he'd almost always gotten his butt kicked, but he'd never once backed down.

Judging by his conversation with Dewayne Millsap, Nathan was still just as stubborn. But Shelby doubted he'd be the underdog in a skirmish nowadays. He looked strong, capable, almost formidable in the darkness as he stared down at her.

He'd turned out to be an attractive man, from what she could see. She wondered what he thought of her.

He grinned suddenly, as if reading her mind. "Look at you, all grown up."

"I should hope so," she said dryly. "I'm thirty years old."

"Where did the time go?" he said softly.

"It…vanished." *Just like my monster.*

He tipped his head slightly, gazing down at her. "I heard you were living out on the west coast. What brings you back here?"

"I came to help my grandmother," Shelby said. "She broke her hip."

"Yeah, I heard about that, too. Is she going to be okay?"

"The doctors think she'll make a full recovery, but she'll be out of commission for quite some time. She asked me to come back and run the shop for her."

"Why not your uncle James?"

"He's a busy man," Shelby said. There was no need for further elaboration, because Nathan knew as well as she that James Westmoreland was not a man who could be trusted, not even by his own mother. That was why Annabel had been compelled to call Shelby for help.

James was so much younger than Shelby's father that he was more like a cousin or an older brother in age, but he and Shelby had never been close. When Shelby had first come to live with her grandmother, her uncle's coldness had hurt her feelings, but she'd learned to stay out of his way. Everything had been okay for a while, but then James had gone and told that awful lie, claimed the monster sighting had been his idea so the family business could profit from the influx of tourists. He'd been willing to tarnish his own reputation in order to defame a nine-year-old girl, and to this day, Shelby didn't understand why.

Nathan had fallen silent, and she followed his gaze across the yard. They were bringing the body up the bank. The stretcher was covered, but Shelby couldn't bear to look. She turned her gaze instead to the river. The water looked iridescent, shimmering like an opal in the moonlight. On the far side, trees crowded the bank, and the fronds of a weeping willow trailed like fingers across the glassy surface.

She wrapped her arms around her middle, shivering in the warm June night. "Why don't you believe it was an accident?" she asked softly.

Nathan glanced at her in surprise, as if he'd forgotten her presence. "What?" Then, shrugging, he said, "It doesn't add up. A lot of things don't add up around here."

"Such as?"

He hesitated. "Maybe I'm just being paranoid."

He didn't strike her as the paranoid type, but then, she hadn't known him since they were kids. "You mentioned Takamura earlier."

"Yeah. Do you remember him?"

"Vaguely." Shelby remembered one afternoon coming back home after a day on the river with Nathan. Her grandmother was sitting on the front porch, clearly upset, as a long, black car pulled away from the house.

"What's the matter, Grandmother?" Shelby asked worriedly.

"That man!" Her grandmother's tone was scathing. "He thinks he can barter for anything he pleases, but I've got news for him. Some things around here just aren't for sale!"

Only recently, Shelby's grandmother had mentioned Takamura again. She'd said he was still trying to buy the supply of freshwater pearls she'd acquired from a man named Wilson Tubb years ago. Most of the jewelry she sold in her shop now was made from pearls that came from the original collection, although she still bought from a few local divers. But the river pearls were almost gone now because the mussel beds had been so badly depleted by pollution and by dredging by people like Takamura.

"He takes and takes and takes," Annabel had said with scorn. "But one of these days, the river is going to claim a price."

Maybe it already had, Shelby thought, glancing at the shrouded stretcher being loaded into the hearse.

She could feel Nathan's gaze on her and she glanced up at him. "You're still a reporter, I take it."

He shrugged. "Some might say that's debatable. I work at the *Argus* now."

"Your uncle's paper?" Memories of past headlines flashed through Shelby's mind. Virgil Dallas had pursed her relentlessly after her monster sighting that night. His stories had drawn reporters from all over the country, had made her a celebrity, but like everyone else in town, he'd turned on her after James had told his lies. "Why did you come back to Arcadia?" she asked Nathan. "As I recall, you couldn't wait to get away from this place."

Something flickered in his eyes, an emotion Shelby couldn't define. "Things change."

"Yes," she agreed quietly. "They do."

He paused, his gaze deep and unfathomable in the moonlight. "I've thought about you over the years, Shelby. Wondered where you were, how you were doing."

The way he said her name sent a soft shiver up her spine. "I've thought about you, too," she admitted.

"Have you?" He sounded surprised. "It's funny, isn't it, how the more things change, the more they stay the same? Look at us. For years we lived on opposite sides of the country, thousands of miles apart. And yet here we both are. Back where we started."

''Full circle,'' Shelby murmured. ''Maybe it's fate.''

''Yeah,'' he said, smiling. But there was an edge of bitterness in his voice when he added, ''Fate can play some pretty strange tricks all right.''

NATHAN CLIMBED into his Bronco and waited for the procession of police cars and the hearse to pull out so that he could fall in line behind them. From his rearview mirror, he could see Shelby standing in the yard, gazing after them. He couldn't see her face in the darkness, but the way she lingered on the lawn, looking a little lost, reminded him of the way she'd seemed that first summer she'd come to live with her grandmother.

Mentally he calculated the years, shocked again to realize how much time had passed since he'd last seen her. And yet the moment he'd heard her name, he'd felt that old, tingling sensation along his backbone. That old awareness.

She'd been nine that first summer, and Nathan had been ten. Older, wiser, he'd naturally stepped into the role of her protector, even though they'd been about the same size—and both small for their ages at that.

Shelby was still petite. When they'd stood talking, she hadn't even come up to his chin. And she'd seemed frail somehow, as if maybe life hadn't been exactly kind to her. The notion made Nathan a little sad because he'd always imagined Shelby Westmoreland living a charmed life, maybe because he'd never gotten over his first impression of her.

In his mind, he could still see her sitting so prim

and proper on Miss Annabel's front porch, nibbling a strawberry ice-cream cone that was the exact color of her dress. Even in the shade of the porch, her blonde hair had shone like new money, and her eyes were wide and clear, forget-me-not blue.

Nathan had been out fishing that day. His bare feet were muddy, and his clothes reeked of the river. To this day, he remembered how daintily Shelby's perfect little nose had turned up in displeasure as he climbed the porch steps and held up a string of catfish for Miss Annabel's inspection.

"Nathan, this is my granddaughter, Shelby. She's going to be staying here with me this summer. I'm very lucky to have her, but I'm afraid she might get a mite lonely, what with just the two of us out here. How about you come around every chance you get and help me keep her company?"

"Okay," he'd mumbled, tongue-tied, having not the faintest idea how one entertained such a creature.

But to Nathan's amazement, he and Shelby had become best friends that summer. In spite of her delicate appearance, she'd been game for almost anything. The pink dress had soon given way to shorts and shirts that had grown, under his expert tutelage, almost as ragged and disreputable as his own clothing.

He'd taught her how to dig for worms in Miss Annabel's flower beds, how to bait a hook, where to find the best fishing holes. He'd taught her how to clean a catfish and how to cook it over a campfire. How to run a trotline. How to dive. Where the currents were safest to swim and where they weren't. He'd shown her his hidden spot—a secret he would have guarded with his life, if necessary—for finding the highly coveted mussels. He'd taught her everything he knew about the river, and then some. All the while, he'd kept his adoration to himself—then, and as they'd grown older—because he'd always been afraid that if she'd suspected his true feelings, she would be so embarrassed and disgusted that she would never want anything to do with him again.

Starting his ignition, Nathan turned on his lights as the last police car moved in behind the hearse. But he didn't put the Bronco in gear because he couldn't quite tear his gaze from the rearview mirror. It came to him, as he watched Shelby in the mirror, that she had seemed like a woman who was badly frightened of something.

Of what? Surely that summer night had long since faded from her memory. There were no monsters, nothing to be afraid of here. Not for her.

But the old protective instinct rose in Nathan anyway, and he had to fight the urge to swing his truck around and go back to make sure she was safe.

He tightened his grip on the wheel. They were adults now, and Shelby was a married woman. A lot of years had passed since he'd tried to slay dragons for her. And monsters. He was out of practice, and besides, the boy who had once had such chivalric tendencies had grown up to be a man with weaknesses of his own.

A man too flawed to be anyone's hero.

NOT UNTIL the last flash of red taillights disappeared around the bend in the road did Shelby turn and start across the yard toward the house.

Police cars. A violent death. Not exactly a desirable welcome home. Certainly not a scenario she would have chosen.

Halfway across the lawn she hesitated, glancing up at the house. Rising on stilts, the looming white structure, so charming by daylight, had always seemed a little spooky to Shelby in the darkness. It wasn't so much the house itself that was eerie as the area beneath. Enclosed in whitewashed latticework, the spider-infested space was used to store everything from garden tools to trunks of old schoolbooks.

Once upon a time, Shelby and Nathan had commandeered the enclosure as a secret clubhouse. But after that fateful summer night, Shelby had considered that cool, smelly dankness a prime hiding place for her monster. She wouldn't go near it.

Even now, she could almost feel eyes staring at her from the darkness, and she hurried up the porch steps, resisting the impulse to glance down. Or over her shoulder at the river.

A light shone through the lace curtain at the front door, and Shelby breathed a sigh of relief. Her grandmother had said Aline Henley had been keeping an eye on the place since the accident and had come by today to tidy up and stock the refrigerator. Annabel must have cautioned Aline to leave a light on for Shelby.

Using her grandmother's key, she opened the door and stepped inside, glancing around at the familiar surroundings. This was better, she thought. Homey. Comforting. Nothing the least bit frightening in here.

Everything was exactly the way she remembered it, although the plank flooring was a little duller, the furniture a little shabbier. But with her grandmother's touch almost everywhere, it still felt more like home than any place Shelby had ever lived with her parents.

The living room was to her left, a long, narrow area decorated with an old-fashioned settee, velvet tufted chairs and a Tiffany-style lamp that gave off a soft, greenish glow. There were ferns everywhere, hanging at the windows that looked out on the river and in terra-cotta frogs and turtles flanking the brick fireplace. The fronds stirred gently under the ceiling fan, and the sluggish movement, coupled with the verdant lamp glow, gave the room an odd, underwater feel that Shelby had never noticed before.

Leaving the front door open, she went back out to the car to get her bags. The scent of the river followed her back inside. Setting her suitcases in the hallway, Shelby turned quickly to close and lock the door as a sense of aloneness settled over her.

She wondered if Nathan was still her nearest neighbor, and wished suddenly that she had asked him earlier if he was living in his father's house. Knowing that Nathan was nearby had once been a great comfort to Shelby.

But he was right. Things had changed since then.

She recalled what he'd said about fate playing strange tricks. His words disturbed her, not because of the melancholia they invoked, but because of the edge of bitterness she'd heard in his voice. The hardness she'd glimpsed in his eyes. When she'd thought about Nathan Dallas over the years, she'd pictured him traveling the world, living the fascinating, adventurous life he'd always seemed destined for.

As a kid, Shelby couldn't imagine how he could ever top diving for pearls. It had seemed like the most romantic profession in the world to her then, and she'd thought Nathan just about the bravest, most exciting person she'd ever known. She'd suffered from a bad case of hero worship that first summer, but, of course, she hadn't let him know that. He'd been too full of himself as it was.

As Shelby had grown older and learned more about the pearling industry from her grandmother, she'd come to understand what a truly grueling occupation diving was. And dangerous, with the river's treacherous currents and all the fishing nets and lines to contend with.

Not to mention loggerhead turtles, she thought with a smile. Those particular bottom-feeders had been Nathan's secret terror, he'd once confided.

She'd liked knowing that even Nathan Dallas was afraid of something.

Picking up her bags, Shelby carried them upstairs and down the hallway to her old bedroom. An alcove of windows, draped with lace, looked out on the river, and almost against her will, Shelby crossed the room and stood staring out at the water.

After a moment, she started to turn away, but a movement on the water stilled her. A series of circles, undulating in the moonlight, grew wider and wider until they lapped gently at the bank.

Chapter Three

"Nathan? You got a minute?" Virgil Dallas's booming voice carried over the usual pandemonium of the newsroom. He stood in the doorway of his office, and when Nathan glanced up from his monitor, his uncle motioned him inside.

Clearing his computer screen, Nathan smothered a groan. In the three months since his uncle had offered him a partnership in the paper, Nathan had had difficulty asserting his autonomy as editor. He'd entered the relationship on one contingency: that he be allowed complete editorial freedom. He would run the newsroom while Virgil would remain at the helm as publisher and business manager.

But Virgil couldn't quite relinquish control. He'd managed every aspect of the paper for over thirty years, and he couldn't help offering unsolicited advice on everything from the editorials to the obits.

His uncle's obstinacy sometimes grated on Nathan's nerves, but he knew he had to suck it up for one very good reason. He had nowhere else to go. He'd once been an award-winning reporter for one of the most respected newspapers in Washington,

D.C., but by the age of thirty, he was finished. Unemployable. A has-been. A freelance hack for the tabloids because no reputable newspaper in the country would touch him after one of his stories had been repudiated as a fraud. He'd trusted the wrong source, and just like that, his career was over.

The partnership with his uncle was Nathan's last chance to prove his journalistic worth, to redeem not just his career and reputation, but his self-respect.

But working at the *Argus* was proving to be more of a challenge than Nathan had anticipated. For one thing, he'd been astounded to learn how poorly managed the paper had been in the last few years as Virgil's age and flagging health had taken a toll. Circulation and ad sales were at an all-time low, and the paper relied much too heavily on filler—stories picked up from news services—with no real reporting. If the trend couldn't be reversed, the *Argus* was destined to go the way of so many small-town newspapers. First, they would have to cut back from a daily circulation to weekly, and then perhaps fold altogether.

Nathan couldn't allow that to happen. He'd poured every last cent he had into the partnership, but it was more than just financial ruin he had at stake here.

He stuck his head inside his uncle's office. "You wanted to see me?"

"Close the door." Virgil leaned back in his chair and folded his hands behind his head as Nathan took a seat across from his desk.

At sixty, his uncle was still an impressive-looking man. Tall and muscular, with keen eyes and a thoughtful, if sometimes mulish, disposition, he had the same world-weary air Nathan had seen on editors and publishers of much larger publications. His hair was completely gray and his face heavily lined by a lifetime of deadlines, pressure and—Nathan suspected—hard drinking. He wouldn't be the first Dallas to succumb to the temptation of the bottle.

"I heard about Danny Weathers at the diner this morning," Virgil said grimly.

Nathan nodded. "I was with the Buford boys last night when they found the body."

His uncle unfolded his hands and placed them on the desk, leaning toward Nathan intently. "I heard that, too. What were you thinking, son? What in the holy hell were you doing out on the river with that pair of lowlifes?"

As always, Nathan grew a little defensive. "I had my reasons. Besides, I'm a grown man. You don't have to worry about bad influences anymore."

"Hell, it's too late to worry about that," Virgil blurted.

"Yeah, I'm a lost cause," Nathan agreed.

As if regretting his harsh words, Virgil's expression softened. "If I thought you were a lost cause, you wouldn't be here, son."

"I appreciate that." Nathan paused, then prompted, "So, is that what you wanted to see me about?"

"Partly. I wanted to find out what you knew about the accident."

"Not much. Only that I seem to be the only one who isn't convinced it *was* an accident. I hope Sheriff McCaid has the good sense to treat this case as a homicide."

"Homicide?" Virgil looked as if the word were almost foreign to him. "Why would he do that?"

"It's standard procedure. Evidence could be destroyed or lost if he waits for the autopsy results." Nathan glanced at his uncle. "Of course, maybe that's the whole point."

Virgil gave him a long, worried appraisal. "This isn't Washington, D.C., son. There's not some 'vast conspiracy' behind every accident." He put quotation marks in the air with his fingers. "You've got to learn to think like a small-town newspaperman, not like some hotshot city reporter. If you don't, you're apt to make yourself some real enemies around here."

"Isn't that the purpose of the fourth estate?" Nathan argued. "To be cynical? To question motives? We're supposed to be the public's watchdog, not some cuddly pet who rolls over and plays dead." He leaned forward in his chair, as if to stress his point. "You can bet I'm going to be all over this story, no matter who I tick off. If Danny Weathers was murdered, I won't rest until his killer is exposed."

Virgil sighed, running a hand through his gray hair. "Look, son, you're the editor now, and far be it for me to tell you how to do your job. But if you ask me, there's another story right in your own backyard you ought to be focusing on."

Nathan lifted a brow. "Which is?"

"Shelby Westmoreland. I hear she's back."

That tingle again at the very mention of her name. Nathan said carefully, "Yeah, she's back. I saw her last night. But her name's August now. She's married."

"No, she's widowed."

"She is?" Nathan tried to keep his tone neutral, but the truth was he still hadn't gotten over the shock of seeing her last night. She'd been sixteen when she'd left Arcadia for the last time. Her parents had come for her after yet another reconciliation, but Nathan had consoled himself with a certainty that she'd soon return. Her parents would split up again, as they always did, and Shelby would be shipped back to her grandmother.

But months had passed, and then a year. Eventually, even her letters had stopped. Nathan had finally become convinced that he would never see her again.

But there she'd stood last night, looking a little too much like the girl he'd never been able to forget.

And now his uncle had informed him that she was a widow. What kind of person would feel happy about that?

"How long has her husband been dead?" he heard himself ask.

"Just over a year. He was murdered."

A shock wave rolled through Nathan. "My God, what happened?"

Virgil shrugged. "Best I recollect, he owned some kind of restoration business. Antiques, I think. He was working alone in his office when a gunman walked in, made him open the safe and then shot him dead. Shelby was the one who found the body."

"Damn." No wonder she'd seemed so fragile last night. So frightened.

Virgil nodded, his expression sober. "That was bad enough, but it got worse. Turned out she'd seen the killer driving away when she pulled into the parking lot. She was able to give the police a description. Even remembered part of the license plate under hypnosis. There was an all-out manhunt for a man named Albert Lunt, but he managed to elude the police for weeks. Then Lunt started making threats toward Shelby.''

''What kind of threats?''

''You name it. He made phone calls. Stalked her. The police even suspected he killed her dog, maybe as a warning, maybe because he was just one sick S.O.B. She was assigned protection, but eventually Lunt made his move. He broke into her house one night and waited for her with a knife. The police officer outside heard her scream and came running, but not before Lunt attacked her. Cut her pretty badly from what I heard, but she must have fought him like a demon, or he would have killed her. The cop shot him, but the wound was superficial. Lunt stood trial a few months later and was convicted of first-degree murder.''

''And Shelby?''

''She was in the hospital for a while. Annabel went out to California to be with her. She told her neighbor, Aline Henley, the girl was a mess, more so emotionally than physically.''

''I don't doubt it,'' Nathan muttered. He didn't want to think about Shelby in the hospital, fighting for her life. He didn't want to think of her terrified, at the mercy of a brutal killer. He liked to remember her in that pink dress, sitting on her grandmother's front porch.

He glanced at his uncle. ''As fascinating as all this is, I don't see what difference it makes. You said it happened over a year ago. It's not news. Where's the story?''

"The story is not what happened to Shelby out in L.A.,'' Virgil said impatiently. "It's what happened to her here.''

"You mean the monster sighting? Come on. That isn't news, either. Besides, James Westmoreland said he concocted the whole thing for profit. You printed his confession yourself.''

Virgil shook his finger at Nathan, a habit he had when he wanted to drive home a point—or browbeat Nathan into doing something he didn't want to. "Listen to me, son. It doesn't matter if she saw a monster that night or not. It doesn't matter if she saw *anything*. What matters is that she became a celebrity. Her story was carried by major newspapers all over the country. She was even on the 'Tonight' show. You don't think people would be interested in finding out what happened to the little girl who cried monster?''

Something stirred in the pit of Nathan's stomach. Revulsion mixed with anger. "Are you suggesting we exploit Shelby's personal tragedy for the sake of some human-interest piece? That isn't reporting. It's gossip. Tabloid journalism.''

"With which you aren't unfamiliar,'' Virgil was quick to point out.

Nathan counted to ten, reminding himself that he owed his uncle more than he could ever repay him. If he had to take a little ego-bashing once in a while, so be it.

Virgil eyed him sagely. "What I'm trying to say is that you're chasing a pipe dream when you go after

Takamura. You think you're going to uncover some big exposé out there on the river that will put you back where you were three years ago, but that's not going to happen. That part of your life is over."

"I realize that," Nathan said through gritted teeth.

Virgil stared at him for a moment. "I'm not sure you do. The *Argus* is a chance for you to start over, rebuild your life. But you have to realize, things are different down here. Priorities are different. Takamura Industries helps put food on the table for a lot of folks in this town, so they don't much care what's going on inside that lab. But Shelby Westmoreland…why, hell, son. She once claimed she saw the Pearl River Monster."

Thinking of the *Argus* as his last chance rather than as a stepping-stone had been a bitter pill for Nathan to swallow. He still had a hard time imagining himself covering weddings and funerals and family reunions for the rest of his life. He couldn't help wanting back what he'd once had. The excitement, the drama, the accolades from his peers. Everything that he'd so carelessly and shamelessly tossed away three years ago.

But his uncle was right. That part of his life was over, and things were different down here. As editor of the town's only newspaper, Nathan had a duty and a responsibility to the community that he couldn't afford to take lightly. He couldn't just go after the stories that suited his purposes, the ones he deemed newsworthy. Building the *Argus* into a paper he could be proud of couldn't come at the expense of his readers. He had to give them what they wanted.

And whether he liked it or not, in Arcadia, Shelby Westmoreland's return was news.

LIKE FAIRY DUST, the treasures inside the Pearl Cove had always cast a spell on Shelby. Made from the finest gold and silver, her grandmother's creations were truly breathtaking, but the focal point of each piece, the absolute stars of the shop were the magnificent freshwater pearls that came in shapes and sizes as varied as their delicate colors—cream, peach, pink, lavender, gold, and more rarely, blue.

Each piece and each pearl was an exquisite work of art, but the blue gems had always been Shelby's favorite, perhaps because they were so rare and so highly coveted.

With a sigh, she tried to rein in her fascination. There was a lot of work to do in the office, and very little time in which to do it. Shelby had come in early to try and reacquaint herself with the shop's operating procedures and accounting methods before the start of business at ten o'clock. As much as she would like to examine leisurely each enticing piece in the display cases, there were more pressing concerns at the moment.

Annabel's faith in Shelby had touched her deeply, but she also had her misgivings about running the shop. She hadn't worked in retail in a long time. But with her previous experience at the Pearl Cove and her accounting knowledge in general, she felt fairly confident she would be able to hold down the fort, at least until her grandmother could return to work.

If she returned, Shelby thought with a pang. The injury, sustained from a fall down the porch steps, had taken a toll. It had been over a year since she'd seen her grandmother, and Shelby had been shocked yesterday to find how much Annabel had aged in that time, how frail she now seemed. What would happen if she could never return to work, if she would always need someone to look after her?

Was Shelby prepared to move back to Arcadia permanently?

It wouldn't be easy. She no longer had a job to worry about since she'd resigned her position at a small, independent film studio, but her home was still in L.A. Michael was buried there. How could she *not* go back? How could she move thousands of miles away without feeling as though she'd somehow betrayed him? Abandoned him?

Rationally, she knew that wouldn't be the case, but her emotions were a different matter. She wasn't ready to let go yet. She couldn't.

Concentrate! she chided herself. With an effort, Shelby put her mind back to the task at hand, scanning the numbers on the computer screen. Recent natural disasters befalling the Japanese cultured-pearl farms had enhanced the desirability of American freshwater pearls, and it appeared that her grandmother had utilized this demand to great advantage. Not only had she increased the size and distribution of her catalogue, she had also added online shopping to the Pearl Cove's web site. The supply of gems on hand, many of them worth several thousand dollars, would allow the shop to maintain the same level of prosperity for years to come, even with the growing scarcity of mussels.

The inventory alone would be worth a small fortune on the current market. Shelby couldn't help but admire her grandmother's keen business acumen. No wonder the shop rested on such a secure financial foundation.

"I see you're wasting no time."

The deep voice startled Shelby. She jumped slightly as her gaze shot up to meet her uncle's. He stood in the doorway, arms folded, impeccably dressed in an expensive gray suit as he glared across the office at her.

The front door was still locked. How had he got in? Shelby wondered. Had her grandmother given him a key, even though she'd admitted to Shelby that she no longer trusted him?

Shelby wasn't surprised. She hadn't trusted her uncle James since his lie had made her a laughingstock in this town. She'd learned only to well what he was capable of, especially where she was concerned.

She hadn't seen him in more than five years, and the fact that he didn't appear to have aged a day was a startling and disturbing contrast to the deterioration Shelby had seen in her grandmother.

Tall, slender, with sun-kissed hair and piercing blue eyes, James, at forty-one, was a striking-looking man who'd left in his wake a long line of soured business deals as he'd drifted carelessly through life, looking for easy money. He wasn't all that different from his older brother, Richard. Shelby's father was a successful stockbroker in California, but after the final breakup with her mother, he'd gravitated from one marriage to another, searching, it seemed, for something that always eluded him.

Shelby's grandmother was the very salt of the earth, kind and generous to a fault. How her two sons could have turned out the way they had was a puzzle to Shelby.

With pantherlike grace, James moved across the room toward her. He stopped at the desk, placing his hands on the glossy surface as he leaned toward her. "Look at you, already settled in Mother's office."

"I'm here because she asked me to come." Shelby refused to let her uncle intimidate her. After all she'd been through, a small-time hustler like James hardly seemed a threat.

Still, there was something about the way he stared at her, the way his lips curled upward in the softest of sneers that chilled her blood. His hatred for her was almost a tangible thing, and such a powerful emotion couldn't be ignored. Whether she wanted to admit it or not, her uncle frightened her. He always had.

"Oh, I don't doubt she asked you to come," he said coolly. "You were always her favorite. You made certain of that."

Shelby frowned. "I don't know what you're talking about."

"Always the innocent. Poor little Shelby, all alone because her parents didn't want her. Poor little Shelby, moping around the house, playing on sympathies, worming her way into a lonely widow's good graces."

"For God's sake, I was nine years old!" Shelby said in astonishment. "You can't honestly think I was that devious."

"Oh, I never underestimated you." He straight-

ened from the desk as she rose to face him. "I still
don't."

"Why?" Shelby forced herself to walk around the
desk, challenging him on his own turf. "Why do you
hate me?"

"Because you're Shelby," he said with a casual
shrug.

She lifted her chin, gazing up at him. "I never did
anything to you."

He gave a low, bitter laugh. "You did plenty, by
God. But if you think I'm going to let you waltz in
here and take what's rightfully mine, you're in for a
very nasty surprise."

Her initial impression of him had been wrong,
Shelby realized. He *had* changed. He was even more
dangerous than she remembered, and she would be
a fool to underestimate *him*.

"I'm here because Grandmother wants me here,"
she said with an edge of defiance. "There's nothing
you can do about it."

"Oh, no?" He grabbed her suddenly, and Shelby
gasped, more in surprise than pain. "You've seen
Mother recently. She's old and frail, and I don't just
mean physically. Her mind's going. With the right
incentive, I think the courts could be persuaded to
find her incompetent."

"You wouldn't," Shelby said in horror. "Even
you couldn't be that cruel. There's nothing wrong
with Grandmother's mind, and you know it."

"Then how come she put a nutcase like you in
charge of her business?"

Shelby's heart thudded against her chest. What did
he mean? What did he know?

He grinned, as if reading her mind. "I know your dirty little secret, Shelby. You had to be hospitalized after you were attacked by your husband's killer. You were sent to the psychiatric ward, weren't you?"

Shelby gasped. "How did you know that?"

"I have my ways. I know a lot of things about you, Shelby. You'd be surprised. You went a little crazy, the way I heard it. Saw monsters everywhere." He paused, smiling, enjoying himself. "They still talk about you at that hospital, you know. The nurses still remember your screams, your little sleepwalking excursions."

So he'd been to the hospital. He'd talked to the people who had cared for her. But why? To use the information against her somehow?

Shelby closed her eyes briefly. She had no wish to be reminded of that time, to revisit the terror of those nightmares, but James's taunts had already opened the wounds.

She tried to struggle away from him, but his grasp tightened. Out of the corner of her eye, she saw a movement in the doorway. A man's voice said sharply, "What's going on in here?"

James released her as suddenly as he'd grabbed her, and Shelby staggered back a step. Nathan was instantly by her side, steadying her. He towered over them both. James had once seemed enormous to Shelby, but now she realized that he was only an average-sized man. A bully who was suddenly dwarfed in Nathan's powerful presence.

"The front door was open. When I came in I heard voices back here. Are you okay?" Nathan asked

Shelby. He held her arm gently, but Shelby winced at the tenderness of her skin.

He turned slowly back to James. "I'll ask you again. What's going on?"

James shrugged, his expression suddenly benign. He smoothed his hand down his silk tie. "A little family powwow. Nothing for you to be concerned about. Unless, of course, you're looking to turn a family squabble into front-page news."

"Shelby?"

Nathan was looking to her for confirmation of James's explanation. All she had to do was say the word and he would take care of her uncle. He would defend her just as ferociously as he had when they were children. Shelby didn't know how she knew this, but she did.

She also knew that she couldn't draw Nathan into her personal problems. She had to find a way to deal with James on her own.

"He's right," she said, glancing up in time to see her uncle's smirk. "We were having a business discussion."

Nathan didn't look as if he bought it for a second, but there was very little he could do under the circumstances. "Well," he said, his gaze troubled, "if you're finished, there's something I'd like to discuss with you, too."

"We aren't finished," James said smoothly. "Not by a long shot. But the rest can wait. I've always been a patient man."

His smile didn't fool Shelby one bit. Nor did it deceive Nathan. His eyes narrowed as James walked over and patted Shelby's shoulder.

"We'll talk again real soon, Shelby, honey. In the meantime, you take care. I worry about you out there on the river, all by your lonesome. You always were scared of your own shadow." His laughter was soft and mocking as he turned and headed for the door. He said over his shoulder, "Now, you call me if you see that monster again, you hear?"

Chapter Four

"What the hell was that all about?" Nathan demanded before James barely had time to get through the door.

"He's just upset that Grandmother put me in charge." Shelby tried to shrug off the incident, but Nathan could see she was still shaken. Her face was pale, and her eyes glittered just a little too brightly. She walked out to the showroom, as if to assure herself that James had really left. Nathan followed her. "He's worried about the business, I guess."

"Worried about getting his hands on Miss Annabel's money, you mean." Nathan had never liked James Westmoreland, and after that summer when he'd made Shelby's life a living hell, Nathan had hated him even more.

He'd never known the full truth of what happened down by the river that night—what Shelby had actually witnessed—though he'd never doubted for a minute that she'd seen something. But after James had claimed that he'd made the whole thing up and gotten Shelby to go along with him, everyone in town—the whole country, it seemed—had ended up laughing at her.

Nathan would have taken great pleasure in pounding James Westmoreland into a bloody pulp, but he'd only been a kid and James had been a grown man. He would have throttled Nathan if given half a chance, but things were different now. If James ever so much as laid a hand on Shelby again...

Nathan drew a deep breath, trying to quell the gnawing urge to go track James down right now and settle that old score. But he didn't think Shelby would welcome his interference. She didn't seem too happy about his presence in general.

He thought about what he'd overheard James say to her—that she'd been hospitalized after her attack. That the nurses still remembered her screams. Those bleak images ate at Nathan. He hated to think of Shelby so vulnerable, alone and frightened.

She'd been through something pretty horrible, and yet here she was, a survivor, a woman with more inner strength than probably even she knew.

Virgil was right. Her story would make a hell of a human-interest piece.

"So what brings you by so early?" She toyed with the filmy scarf tied at her neck. The blue floral pattern brought out the azure of her eyes and the creamy quality of the pearls in her lobes. Her hair was cut in a short, choppy style that looked as if she'd taken the shears to it in desperation, but that had, in reality, probably cost a fortune at some exclusive Beverly Hills salon. She looked both elegant and sophisticated standing behind a display case, and it struck

Nathan anew how many years had come and gone since he'd last seen her.

He moved around to the other side, so they were standing face-to-face, with only the expanse of the glass case between them. "It's been a long time since we've seen each other, and we didn't get much of a chance to talk last night."

"No, I guess we didn't." She paused, her gaze anxious. "Have you heard anything more about the body they found in the river?"

"Not much. His name was Danny Weathers."

She nodded. "Yes, Dewayne told me last night. The name sounds familiar."

"He was my age. We used to hang out sometimes." Nathan frowned, remembering Danny Weathers as a boy, the times they'd gone fishing together, camped out on the river together. Nathan had used their childhood friendship as a way to reconnect with Danny once he'd found out Danny worked for Takamura. Now Danny was dead, and Nathan had a bad feeling—a very bad feeling—that it might be because Danny had talked to him. If that was the case, it was as Nathan had told his uncle—he wouldn't rest until the truth came out.

Shelby gazed at him strangely, as if she'd somehow picked up on his thoughts. "You're still not convinced it was an accident, are you?"

"Let's just say I'm keeping an open mind." He glanced down at the jewelry pieces and the assortment of loose pearls protected inside the glass. "Your grandmother still does beautiful work, doesn't she?"

Shelby smiled. "Do you remember what we used to call some of the shapes of the pearls?"

"Angel wings, rosebuds, turtlebacks, dog's teeth." Nathan grinned. "Strange how it all comes back. I always figured pearlers gave the baroque shapes such colorful names to add to their mystique, since they were less valuable than the rounds."

"Very possibly." Shelby unlocked the case and took out a cream-colored pearl with a magnificent luster. Nested in her hand, the gem came alive, glowing like moonlight against her palm. "Grandmother always said pearls are like candlelight. So romantic and very flattering, no matter the skin tone."

"I agree." Nathan took the pearl from Shelby's hand, lifting it to her face.

The pearl felt cool against his fingertips, a fine counterpoint to the warmth of Shelby's smooth cheek. He hadn't touched her in a very long time, and the feel of her skin against his, the knowledge that she was so close after all these years...

She stepped back suddenly, as if she'd been burned. The pearl would have dropped to the glass surface if Nathan hadn't caught it in time.

Her gaze flew up to meet his. She seemed a little dazed. Nathan wondered what she was thinking, if the touch of his fingers against her cheek had affected her the same way it had him. "Have dinner with me tonight," he said impulsively.

She looked almost shocked. "I...can't."

"Why not?"

"I don't go out."

"Even with an old friend?"

"No." Her tone was adamant.

"I don't understand." Nathan gazed at her for a long, silent moment. "We were once best friends. Why would it be so wrong for us to have dinner together?"

Her expression turned almost defiant, as if she were fighting very hard to control her emotions. "Our friendship was a long time ago."

"Yes, but I haven't had a really close friend since you left town." He paused, then said softly, "I think maybe it's been that way for you, too."

She frowned. "What makes you think I don't have close friends?"

"Because you were always a loner. Just like me."

"Don't assume you still know me," she warned. "People change in twenty years."

Not you, he thought. In spite of the changes in her appearance, Shelby was very much the way he remembered her. Sweet, quiet, very intense. Soft-looking on the outside, but tough on the inside when she had to be.

She'd never been one to run from her fears—even going so far as to wait on the riverbank at midnight for a glimpse of the Pearl River Monster. And then later, when people in town had turned against her, she'd faced the ridicule with the same quiet determination, never once running away. Never once dissolving into tears.

Nathan had been the one to act a fool, swearing at her tormentors, picking fights, getting his nose bloodied more times than he could count. That was what had made Shelby cry.

He gazed at her now, haunted by the pain in her eyes, and he wished fervently that he could have been there the night Albert Lunt had come after her. Wished, even, that he could have saved her husband.

"I'm sorry about your husband," he said softly.

Her gaze faltered. "I don't like to talk about it."

"Then we don't have to. We can talk about anything you like. Think of it as two old friends catching up. We haven't seen each other in years, Shelby. There's a lot I'd like to know about you."

One brow lifted slightly. "Such as?"

"Have dinner with me and I'll tell you." Shelby had never been able to resist a challenge. It had been her downfall more than once. If Nathan hadn't dared her, she never would have gone down to the river that night. "Come on. For old times' sake."

She gave him an exasperated look. "You haven't changed much, have you? You still don't like taking no for an answer."

"Is that a yes, then?" he asked hopefully.

"It'll have to be an early dinner," she finally conceded. "I don't like driving home alone after dark."

"Deal," he agreed, smiling. Feeling triumphant for no good reason. "But don't worry. I wouldn't dream of letting you drive home alone. I'll follow you."

She said nothing to that, but her expression seemed to suggest that his words were hardly reassuring.

SHELBY WAITED until the door closed behind Nathan before hurrying over to the window to watch him stride down the street. The sidewalk was empty this time of morning, but with his looks and bearing, he would have been noticed even in a crowd.

Last night, under cover of darkness, Shelby had thought him attractive, but this morning, in broad daylight, with sunlight gleaming against his dark hair—

She drew a sharp breath.

He was more than attractive. Nathan Dallas had turned out to be a very handsome man. Drop-dead gorgeous, in fact. The single women in town were probably leaving tracks on each other's backs in their haste to capture his attention.

But Shelby wasn't one of them.

Watching him disappear around a corner, she rallied her resolve. She wouldn't be going to dinner with Nathan Dallas tonight or any other night. She'd only agreed in order to quell his persistence. In an hour or so, she'd call the *Argus* and leave a message. She'd say something had come up. She couldn't make it after all.

But the thought of spending the evening alone was hardly tempting, either. Shelby hadn't slept well last night. She wanted to believe the country quiet had kept her awake, but she knew better. The river was a spooky place, had been since that summer night when she'd seen something rise out of the water and start toward her.

Realistically, she knew the Pearl River Monster didn't exist. The vision had been conjured by her imagination and by all the talk that summer about the creature. She'd been just a kid back then, frightened and lonely. It might have been nothing more than shadows in the moonlight that had terrified her. Nothing more than an illusion caused by the darkness. But she *had* seen something.

Over the years, Shelby had managed to look back on that night with an open mind and even with some humor. She'd created quite a stir in Arcadia that summer. The ridicule she'd taken after the *Argus* had declared her sighting a hoax had, in time, taken on comic overtones. The town had turned on her because the national media had made them all look like fools. Shelby accepted that now. She even speculated with some amusement that her monster sighting was what had compelled her to go into accounting instead of the arts, although she'd always had a creative flair. After that summer, she'd wanted to deal in the concrete, not the abstract.

But after Michael had been killed and Albert Lunt had come after her, her logic had deserted her. Entering her darkened house that night, Shelby had sensed Lunt's presence before she'd seen him, and the cold, black, mind-numbing terror of that long-ago summer had come rushing back.

But somehow she'd managed to survive both river monsters and Albert Lunt.

You're stronger than you give yourself credit for, Shelby.

No, I'm not, Dr. Minger. If I were strong, I wouldn't be dreaming about monsters.

The creature in your nightmares is nothing more than a manifestation of Lunt. Your reaction is perfectly understandable.

Was it? Shelby had thought she'd conquered the worst of her fears, but last night, lying wide-awake in the darkness, an uneasiness had come over her she hadn't been able to shake. Had she made a mistake in coming back here? Were the old nightmares from her childhood feeding into the terror Albert Lunt had so deftly instilled in her?

The back of her neck tingled with that same disquiet now, and the realization that she was no longer alone crept over her, and she turned.

The young woman Shelby saw at the back of the store was very lovely, with long black hair and skin so pale as to almost appear translucent. She was tall and willowy in the most ethereal sense of the word, and she'd moved so silently Shelby hadn't heard her come in through the back door.

The girl stood still as a statue, her gaze cast downward as she extended her hand over the water in one of the freshwater aquariums. The fish had all swum to the top, hovering in a shimmering cloud just beneath the surface, as if they'd been drawn there by some irresistible force, some powerful magnet that held them in thrall.

Shelby stood mesmerized herself for a moment. Then she realized who the young woman was and what she was doing. Delfina Boudreaux, another of Annabel's strays, was feeding the fish. The hungry little creatures were gobbling up the minuscule morsels greedily before the food had time to filter down through the water.

Delfina was so absorbed in her task, she hardly seemed aware of another presence, and Shelby took a moment to study her. She knew the girl was no more than eighteen or nineteen. Her grandmother had told her that Delfina had been orphaned when she was thirteen, and she'd lived all alone in a tumbledown shack by the river, eluding the authorities so she wouldn't be sent to a foster home, and surviving on instincts and handouts until she'd turned sixteen. Then Annabel had given her a job.

Shelby walked across the room toward the girl and extended her hand. "Hello. I'm Shelby August, Miss Annabel's granddaughter. You must be Delfina."

The girl's gaze lifted from the fish tank, and a shiver of unease rippled along Shelby's spine. There was something strange about Delfina Boudreaux, a knowing quality in her deep, mossy-green eyes that seemed both mystic and primal.

Delfina's cool fingers brushed against Shelby's. "I knew you were coming," she said, in a voice that was as soft as the tinkle of crystal wind chimes.

"I'm sure Grandmother mentioned she'd asked me to come here and help out," Shelby said, ignoring her uneasiness. "I hope you don't mind working with a stranger."

A ghost of a smile touched the girl's lips. "You're not a stranger, Shelby."

The way she said her name sent another chill down Shelby's backbone. "But we've never met."

Delfina paused, the green gaze giving Shelby a long, enigmatic appraisal. "Your grandmother speaks of you often."

But Shelby had the distinct impression that it wasn't through Annabel that Delfina had heard of her. Who, besides her grandmother, had been talking about her? Her uncle James?

That notion did little to scuttle Shelby's disquiet. She gazed back at the girl, wondering about her loyalty to Annabel. If Delfina was somehow in cahoots with James it wouldn't bode well for Shelby's future peace of mind.

Don't borrow trouble, her grandmother would advise.

"Well," she said briskly. "I suppose we should get back to work. I'll be in the office if you need me."

There. A subtle reminder of who was in charge here.

But Delfina either didn't notice or didn't care. Seemingly oblivious to Shelby's presence once again, Delfina smiled dreamily, but whether at some internal amusement or at the antics of the neon tetras, only she could say.

Chapter Five

"I wasn't sure you'd come."

Truthfully, Shelby wasn't certain why she had. She'd been set to call the whole thing off, but then Nathan had called her first and suggested they meet at Willie's Boathouse. Somehow, she'd found herself agreeing to his invitation yet again.

Her grandmother used to say that Nathan was blessed with the power of persuasion. "I swear, that boy could be a preacher if he had a mind to."

Nathan Dallas, a preacher? Shelby didn't think so.

Nathan set aside his beer and rose as Shelby approached the table. "I hope you don't mind. I felt like sitting outside."

"No, it's nice."

They both sat, and a waitress immediately came over to take their order. Once the girl had hustled off, Shelby glanced around, searching for a safe topic of conversation. "Do you remember how Grandmother used to bring us here to celebrate my birthday? She'd always call ahead to make sure they had chocolate cake and ice cream, and then after dinner, we'd go see a movie at the old drive-in theater. Later, I'd open my presents out on the front porch.''

Nathan smiled. "It was nice, wasn't it?"

"The best birthdays I ever had were spent here with Grandmother. And with you," she added shyly. "The ones I spent with my parents were some of the loneliest."

"It must have been rough, being bounced around like that." Nathan gazed at her intently, and Shelby found herself shivering, even though the breeze was still warm. The setting sun cast long shadows over the deck, making his eyes seem even darker and more than a little mysterious.

"You didn't have it so easy yourself," she said. "Your mother left you, too."

He shrugged and turned to stare at the river. "I barely remember her."

Shelby didn't think that was true. She suspected he did remember his mother—and her betrayal—all to well. "That's why you didn't come to the river that night, even though we'd planned to meet at midnight. I remember hearing later that your mother had left. Up until then, I was pretty mad at you for standing me up and leaving me to face the monster alone."

He frowned briefly into his beer. "She'd gone off the night before. When I got up that morning, I found my dad sitting at the kitchen table, holding the note and just staring off into space. He couldn't read or write, but I think he had a pretty good idea what the letter said. He just handed it to me without a word."

Shelby had a sudden image of Nathan at ten years old—scrawny, barefoot, always looking for trouble.

He'd been a boy already seasoned by years of grueling work, but still far too young to know how to deal with his mother's abandonment. Too young to have to read a Dear John letter to his own father. She felt something awaken inside her, a tenderness she hadn't felt for anyone in ages. "Have you ever tried to find her?"

Her question seemed to startle him. "No. Why would I?"

"You're a reporter. You have the know-how, the contacts. She's still your mother, Nathan."

"She could be dead for all I know." He said the words flatly, but there was a shadow of pain in his eyes he couldn't quite hide.

"Did your father try to locate her?"

"Not that I know of." He paused for a moment, then shrugged. "I guess in some strange way I always thought it would be a betrayal of him if I tried to look her up. And besides, she's the one who walked out on us. I never thought I had anything to say to her. Anything she'd want to hear, at least."

"You never heard from her at all?"

He glanced at Shelby, his gaze still shadowed with memories. "There were Christmas cards for a while. A birthday present or two. She even called the paper once after I started working there. At least, Virgil said he thought it was her. But she hung up before I could get to the phone. I guess she chickened out or decided she didn't have anything to say to me, either."

"I'm sorry."

"Ancient history." He took a sip of his beer. "So

what about you? I heard your parents split up for good a few years ago."

She wondered where he'd heard that. It gave her a strange feeling to think that Nathan might have asked about her over the years. "Dad's still in L.A., but Mother moved to Seattle a while back. I don't hear much from either one of them."

"Not even when your husband died?"

Shelby felt the cold weight of her sorrow come crashing back down on her shoulders. "Not even then."

"I'm sorry, too." Their gazes met, and for a brief moment, Shelby took comfort in the understanding glimmering in Nathan's eyes, in the shared memories of their past.

The food came then, and they both fell silent as the waitress placed the plates in front of them. Willie's specialized in fresh fish and homegrown vegetables from their own garden. Nathan and Shelby had both ordered the trout, and it came sizzling hot and delicately spiced, with side orders of green beans, sliced tomatoes and corn bread dripping with butter.

"Not your usual L.A. fare of tofu and bean spouts," Nathan remarked wryly.

"It's delicious." Shelby felt ravenous, all of a sudden, as if she hadn't eaten in years. She bit into the corn bread and sighed. "Has real butter always tasted this good?"

"How quickly we forget the simple pleasures."

"Out of sight, out of mind," Shelby agreed.

He stopped eating for a moment and gazed across the table at her. "Is that why you never came back to Arcadia? Because you forgot your life here? You were, what? Sixteen the last time your parents came and got you? You always said you'd move back here permanently as soon as you turned eighteen. Why did you change your mind?''

She laid down her fork, her appetite gone as quickly as it had come. ''Because I met Michael that year,'' she said quietly.

NATHAN FELT as if she'd stuck a knife straight into his gut.

She hadn't come back to Arcadia—to him—because she'd met a man named Michael.

No reason to feel betrayed, he told himself grimly. By the time Shelby had turned eighteen, he'd been long gone from this town himself. And besides, her husband was dead now. Stupid to feel jealous of a dead man, except…when he'd been alive, he'd been married to Shelby. He'd had the one thing that Nathan had always known he could never have.

He'd been her friend, her protector, her rescuer at times. Maybe even her hero. But he'd never been her lover.

He glanced at Shelby now, saw the pain in her eyes and he knew that she had loved her husband deeply. Knew that she still loved him and probably always would.

They didn't talk again for several long minutes. Nathan finished his dinner while Shelby picked at her food. After a while, the waitress came to clear the table as the sun sank lower on the horizon. It would be dark soon. The lightning bugs would be out, and the mosquitoes. Nostalgia worked like a drug on Nathan's sense. He couldn't take his eyes off Shelby.

"What was your husband like?" he heard himself asking.

She looked surprised by the question. "He was a little older than me, but not much. And it never mattered. At least not to me." She paused, as if the memories were too painful to recall. "We met when I was eighteen, but we didn't get seriously involved until I was out of college and had established my career in accounting. His idea, not mine. He wanted to make sure I knew my own mind, but there was never any question for me."

The knife twisted a little deeper in Nathan's stomach. "How long were you married?"

"Almost five years."

"That's a long time."

"Not really. In some ways, it seems like only a moment," she said softly.

But five years *was* a long time to Nathan's way of thinking. He'd always marveled at people's ability to make such a commitment, which was probably why he'd never had a relationship last more than a year or so. In his younger days, he'd been too busy chasing dreams. Then chasing stories. Now he was chasing his past.

Every misstep, every mistake he'd ever made came back to haunt him as he sat across the table from Shelby. She'd been the victim of circumstances. He'd been a man too caught up in his own ambition and self-importance. He'd wanted to change the world with his reporting, but all he'd done in the end was hurt innocent people.

What had Michael August done?

He'd died young, for one thing, with Shelby still

in love with him. That would be a hard act to follow, and Nathan had no desire to be compared to Shelby's dead husband in any respect.

"So what about you?" she asked. "Have you ever been married?"

"No. Never even came close."

She seemed surprised. "Why not?"

Because no one ever quite measured up to you, he thought. Aloud he said, "Too busy, I guess. You know how it is. Things happen. Before you know it, time just slips away from you."

She nodded. "I do know. And speaking of time, it's getting late. I should go home."

"Give me a second to pay the bill, and I'll follow you," Nathan told her.

"That isn't necessary."

"It is for me."

She started to protest again, but then shrugged and turned back to stare at the river. A breeze ruffled her hair and the blue scarf tied around her throat. Nathan wondered if she was thinking about Michael. If she was wishing he was here with her instead of Nathan.

If it was stupid to be jealous of a dead man, he thought bitterly, then it probably wasn't a good idea to hate him.

SHELBY STOOD at the window and watched Nathan's taillights recede in the distance. True to his word, he'd followed her home, but he hadn't walked her to the door. Instead, he'd waited in the drive until she'd gotten safely inside and flipped on several lights before he'd turned his Bronco and headed back toward town. To put in a few more hours at the paper, he'd said.

Shelby wasn't certain whether to feel relieved or disappointed by his hasty departure. In spite of her misgivings, she'd enjoyed their dinner together. Nathan had always been excellent company, and in some ways, very little had changed between them. They could still talk about almost anything with one another, but Shelby knew it would be a mistake to assume that a grown man and woman could have the same relationship they'd enjoyed as kids.

There was the attraction between them, for one thing. Shelby had always had tender feelings toward Nathan, but now her reaction to him was more threatening. More dangerous. More than she wanted to feel for any man right now. Her husband was dead, but that didn't make her any less committed to him. Any less married. How could she simply put aside everything she and Michael had shared in order to move on with someone else?

Maybe in time she would be able to do that. Maybe in the distant future, she'd meet another man, someone kind and gentle who wouldn't threaten Michael's place in her heart.

But Nathan Dallas wasn't that man. Somehow Shelby knew that he would never be content to share her with her husband's memory. He would always want more of her than she was willing to give. It would be best for both of them if they never even started down that road.

"Assuming he's attracted to *you*," Shelby murmured. It was possible all Nathan wanted from her was just what he'd said—dinner with an old friend.

But the way he'd looked at her, his eyes so dark and intense…

Something soft and furry rubbed against Shelby's leg, startling her out of her reverie.

"Why, Miss Scarlett!" she exclaimed, bending down to pick up her grandmother's black cat. "Where did you come from?"

The cat meowed once in response, gazing at Shelby with eyes as green and beguiling as her namesake's.

"How'd you get inside? Did Mrs. Henley bring you home?" Since the cat hadn't been around last night, Shelby had assumed that Aline Henley was caring for her while Annabel was in the hospital.

"Strange she wouldn't leave a note or something," Shelby mused. "Oh, well." Glad of the company, she nuzzled her cheek against Miss Scarlett's sleek, ebony fur. The cat wore a strange, musty scent, as if she'd been locked up in some damp place for a long while. Shelby thought about the area beneath the house, wondering if Miss Scarlett had taken it over as her secret hideaway.

"You don't have a litter of kittens somewhere that I should know about, do you?" She carried the cat into the kitchen and filled her food and water bowls. Miss Scarlett greedily attacked her dinner as if she hadn't eaten in days.

"Poor baby," Shelby murmured, watching the cat scarf down the food. She was still puzzled by Miss Scarlett's sudden appearance. If Aline Henley hadn't brought her home, then how had the cat gotten inside?

Miss Scarlett, however, seemed unconcerned by

Shelby's quandary. Her bowl cleaned, the petite feline set about cleaning herself as delicately as possible, licking her little paws and then rubbing them
against her face. The grooming went on for several
minutes until, immaculate once again, she strutted
over to Shelby and waited, queenlike, to be picked
up.

Shelby happily complied, scratching the cat's neck
absently as she stared out the kitchen window. Darkness had fallen since Nathan left, and that sense of
aloneness crept over her. Miss Scarlett's presence
helped, but Shelby suddenly wished that she'd in-
vited Nathan in for a cup of coffee or a drink, anything to abate the uneasiness stealing over her as the
night outside deepened.

Miss Scarlett, motor gently running, had settled
herself in Shelby's arms, but suddenly the purring
halted and the fur on her back rose in alarm. Her
green gaze shot to the window, where her attention
seemed riveted on the river.

Reluctantly, Shelby followed Miss Scarlett's gaze.
The water was calm, with not so much as a ripple
marring the mirrorlike surface. But as Shelby contin-
ued to watch, she saw something stir down by the
river's edge. A shadow that moved in and out of the
trees.

An animal, she told herself firmly, but she found
herself holding her breath as she leaned toward the
window, trying to peer through the trees.

The movement stopped suddenly, as if the shadow
had sensed Shelby's presence. For one terrible moment, she had the impression of eyes staring at her

through the darkness. Of something malevolent that had spotted her in the window.

Then suddenly the river's smooth surface exploded in a series of rolling circles, as if someone—or something—had dived into the water.

Without realizing it, Shelby's grasp tightened on the cat, and Miss Scarlett gave a frantic cry, digging her claws into Shelby's flesh before leaping from her arms in protest. She was out of the kitchen in a flash, and a split second later, Shelby heard the distant thunder of tiny paws racing up the stairs.

Just what she needed, Shelby thought glumly. A neurotic cat on her hands.

"One crazy in the house is more than enough," she mumbled, before following Miss Scarlett upstairs.

Chapter Six

Sunlight slanted across Shelby's face as she wakened slowly, the remnants of a dream teasing her consciousness. But rather than the instant of terror she normally experienced when coming out of a nightmare, she felt troubled in a way she couldn't name. And then she realized why. She'd been dreaming about Nathan.

They'd been—

Shelby put a hand to her forehead in distress as the erotic visions came back to her. Oh, no! How could she have had *those* thoughts, even subconsciously, about a man other than her husband? It wasn't right.

But even through her guilt, Shelby could rationalize the dream. Michael had been gone for over a year. She was lonely. And then Nathan had turned up in her life so unexpectedly.

Dr. Minger would undoubtedly tell her that her dream was a manifestation of the internal turmoil she'd undergone, not just since Michael died, but in moving back to Arcadia. This place was bound to stimulate powerful memories for her.

But Shelby's logic did little to alleviate her disquiet. She felt as if her own mind had betrayed her by using her emotions to wreak havoc on her sleep.

The best thing to do was simply to put the images out of her mind, she told herself sternly. She wouldn't think about them. She wouldn't dwell on them. She wouldn't, for one moment, consider there might be another reason why she'd dreamed about Nathan. Why the two of them had been—

No!

Shoving the visions firmly aside, Shelby raised herself on her elbows and glanced around, still feeling off-centered. A large volume entitled *The History of the Pearl* lay on the bed beside her, along with her reading glasses, but she had no recollection of having placed them there. She did, however, remember reading until well past midnight, with Miss Scarlett curled nervously at her feet.

The cat was gone now, having disappeared, it would seem, at the first light of day. Back to her secret hideout? Shelby wondered.

They'd both had a bad case of the jitters last night. Seeing shadows. Imagining all sorts of sinister goings-on down by the river.

Stretching, Shelby walked over to the window to stare out. The day was beautiful, with a pure, crystalline-blue sky and high banks of cauliflower clouds hanging motionless over a sun-speckled river. The dream tried to intrude again, but Shelby wouldn't let it. She turned her thoughts instead to Michael.

Mornings were the time when she missed him most. Waking up beside him. Anticipating the day. Sharing a smile and the million and one small touches—a passing caress, the sweep of his hand down her hair, the brush of his fingers against hers— as they readied themselves for work.

"Michael," she whispered, gazing at the river. "Why?"

It was a question that could never be answered, of course. Why did anyone have to be struck down in the prime of life? Why did the good always have to die young?

Why couldn't Shelby have been on time that day? If she'd arrived at the office even fifteen minutes earlier, chances were she and Michael would have been long gone before Lunt arrived.

The last question was the one that tortured her the most, even though the police had disputed her theory. In the course of their investigation, they'd uncovered a disturbing connection after Lunt had been arrested. He'd once worked for a contractor Shelby and Michael had hired to remodel their house. He'd been fired following several complaints they'd made about his work and his conduct, and the police had come to think that Lunt, in his own twisted way, blamed Shelby and Michael for his dismissal and for the subsequent breakup of his family. There was no telling how long he'd been in their lives, lurking on the fringes, waiting to tear their world apart.

So now Michael was dead, but Lunt still lived.

Fingering the scar at her throat, Shelby shivered in the warm sunshine streaming in through the window. A sparrow landed on the window ledge, and she watched it for a moment, grateful for the distraction.

The bird pecked at something on the ledge, then

sensing a human presence, flitted away. But Shelby's gaze remained on the sill where the bird had alighted. The white paint had been stained by what looked like streaks of rusty-brown mud.

Mud? Outside a second-story window?

Curious, Shelby opened the window and pushed out the screen far enough to study the stains. Tentatively, she touched her finger to one of the streaks. The mud was cool and still a bit moist, but when she examined her skin, she saw that it had been stained red, not brown. As if the streaks were...

Blood!

The realization hit her like a freight train, and stunned, Shelby snatched her hand back inside the window, cradling it against her chest as if she were the one who had been wounded. But she was fine. Then...who?

Am image rose in her mind. Weeks before Albert Lunt had broken into her home, he'd gotten into her backyard and poisoned her dog, a sweet little mutt named Vincent. Shelby had never had any proof Lunt was responsible, but she'd known. So had the police. They'd assigned her protection after that, but Lunt had still come after her. He'd taken everything from her, but he still wanted more.

Horrified by the memory, Shelby whirled and ran out of the bedroom, calling to her grandmother's cat as she flew down the stairs. "Miss Scarlett! Miss Scarlett! Where are you?"

Her heart pounding in dread and fear, Shelby opened the front door and raced onto the porch, stopping short when she saw more of the stains on the front steps. Not spatters or drops, but smears, as if something had been dragged down the stairs. Something mortally wounded.

Lunt had carried poor little Vincent from the backyard to Shelby's front porch, where she'd found him when she came home from the grocery store. She'd known at that moment that Lunt would never rest until he got her, too.

"Miss Scarlett! Here, kitty! Where are you?" she called frantically.

In a deep panic, Shelby ran down the steps, then stopped at the bottom, forcing herself to examine the streaks. She was fairly certain the stains were blood mixed with mud. But the yard was completely dry. It hadn't rained in weeks.

Clumps of bloodied fur had been strewn in the grass near the steps. With a quivering stomach, Shelby followed the gruesome trail to the trellis outside her bedroom window.

The body lay on the ground directly below her window. Her stomach recoiled with such horror that for a moment, she could do nothing but avert her gaze and take long, stabilizing breaths. Then she forced her legs to move. Whatever it was—please, not Miss Scarlett—might still be alive. Might need her help.

Shelby knelt beside the trellis. In her mind's eye she saw herself kneeling beside Michael, his warm blood staining her hands crimson, his eyes open and gazing up at her. He'd been alive, but just for a moment. Not long enough, even, for her to tell him she loved him.

Shoving aside the agonizing memories, Shelby gazed down. The carcass was so badly mutilated that it took her a moment to realize it wasn't a cat, but a rabbit. And it was most certainly dead.

She rocked back on her heels, tears filling her eyes. Nothing should have to suffer this way, she thought fiercely. Not Michael, not her little dog, nothing. What kind of animal could be so vicious? What kind of creature could kill so brazenly, and then climb a trellis to gaze inside her bedroom window?

"YOU'RE SURE he couldn't have gotten out?" Sitting in her grandmother's office, Shelby clutched the phone to her ear as she absently sorted through a bin of loose pearls she'd pulled from the vault earlier.

"I'm positive, Shelby. Please try to relax." Dr. Minger, as always, spoke in calm, solacing tones. "I talked to Detective Hagler after you first called me this morning," he said, referring to the homicide detective who had been in charge of Michael's case. "He assured me that Albert Lunt is still in prison. There is absolutely no chance he could have escaped."

Shelby could picture the psychiatrist seated in his deep, leather chair, the bow tie he favored slightly askew, and his teeth clamped around the stem of an ebony pipe he never lit. The image was immediately comforting. It was in Dr. Minger's office, surrounded by all his beloved books, that Shelby had begun to think she might someday be able to put her life back together.

This morning that notion had taken a serious blow.

"Thank you for calling Detective Hagler for me," she said.

"No trouble at all." Dr. Minger paused. "You know, Shelby, there's a perfectly logical explanation for what you found. Didn't you say your grandmother has a cat? Felines are natural predators."

The thought had occurred to Shelby, too, but Miss Scarlett was such a sweet, gentle pet. Shelby hated to think that the cat might have her savage moments as well, but it made sense. Miss Scarlett had killed a rabbit and left it on the grass beneath the bedroom window for Shelby to find. Then she'd climbed the trellis and tried to get back inside the house.

Only one problem with that scenario. When had Miss Scarlett gone outside? Before Shelby had fallen asleep, the cat had been draped over her feet, evidently as unnerved by the darkness as Shelby. It was hard to imagine her venturing out into the night to chase rabbits.

Still, it was more logical than Albert Lunt having escaped from prison and finding his way to Arkansas.

Shelby gave a shaky laugh. "You're probably right. I'm sorry for overreacting."

"Don't apologize for your feelings. I want you to call me any time you need to."

"Thanks."

"So how is everything else going down there?" Shelby could hear the squeak of his chair as he settled more comfortably into the leather. "As I recall, you were anticipating some trouble from your uncle."

Shelby glanced at the various storage containers she'd removed from the vault earlier and stacked on her desk. Inside the bins, the shop's extensive collection of loose pearls had been sorted into compartments according to shape, size and quality. She'd been working on the inventory list all morning, and although admittedly she'd been distracted by what had happened at home earlier, she was afraid she'd detected a problem. Possibly a big one. It appeared that some of her grandmother's most valuable pearls had gone missing.

She said nothing of this to Dr. Minger, however. Business difficulties she could handle on her own. "My uncle may be trying to start some trouble," she allowed, thinking of James's threat to have her grandmother committed, "but I'm not going to let him get away with it."

"Good for you," Dr. Minger said approvingly. "I'm proud of you, Shelby. I think Michael would be, too."

Funny how the mention of her husband's name didn't hurt quite as much as it once had. Was her grief fading along with her memories? Shelby wondered guiltily.

She didn't want to forget Michael. She wanted to remember every moment of their time together, savor every smile, every whisper the two of them had shared.

But last night it hadn't been her husband's smile she'd dreamed about. It hadn't been Michael she'd heard whispering to her, telling her things only a lover would say.

Shelby hadn't dared let herself dwell on those disturbing images since waking up this morning, and once she'd found the dead rabbit, she'd been too upset to think about anything but Lunt.

Now, however, in a calmer moment, the dream

came back to her again, and she wondered if she should mention it to Dr. Minger. But somehow she couldn't bring herself to. The images were too private. Too intimate.

Too disturbing.

Shelby closed her eyes for a moment. She didn't want to think of Nathan Dallas in those terms. He was an old friend, and that was all he would ever be. She couldn't—wouldn't—allow him to become more.

Besides, dreams didn't necessarily mean anything. Shelby still had nightmares about monsters, but that didn't mean they really existed. So what if she'd dreamed last night that Nathan had made love to her? That certainly didn't mean it was ever going to happen.

But it was hard to get the images out of her mind, and after she'd hung up from Dr. Minger, Shelby sat for a long moment, thinking about the dream. About the time she'd spent last evening with Nathan. She couldn't deny he was an attractive man, or that she had feelings for him.

But that was only natural. They'd been inseparable as kids, and a strong bond had been forged between them that first summer. A bond that hadn't been severed even when Shelby's parents had taken her back to California from time to time. Even as she and Nathan had grown older and away from each other.

Shelby had always considered him her best friend, her soul mate, and she'd known that if she were ever in trouble, Nathan would be there for her.

Even after so many years apart, Nathan had been the first person she'd thought of during her crisis following Michael's murder and her attack. Lying awake in the hospital at night, too terrified even to close her eyes, she would think about all those carefree summer days spent with Nathan on the river, the easy camaraderie the two of them had shared. The way he'd always tried to protect her.

Somehow the memories had given her a measure of comfort when nothing else could, and Shelby had been tempted more than once to call him, to ask him to come out to California to be with her.

In the end, she'd convinced herself it wasn't such a good idea because so many years had passed. Nathan had his own life. She wasn't even sure he'd remember her.

But the look in his eyes last night told her that he did remember. Perhaps more than she wanted him to.

"IT'S A REAL BEAUTY, Nathan." Annabel Westmoreland's blue eyes gleamed with admiration as she held the pearl up to the sunlight. "Look at that rosy overtone. Just beautiful!" She gave him a doubtful glance. "Are you sure you want to give it away? The shop would be more than happy to buy it from you."

"Haven't we had this conversation before?" Years ago, Nathan had shyly offered Shelby's grandmother a pearl he'd found in the river for her private collection, and she'd tried to buy that one from him, too. But it had been a gift—the only thing Nathan had owned of any value—to try and repay her for her kindness to him that summer. In the end, she'd accepted it gracefully, giving him a big hug as tears glittered in her eyes.

Nathan pulled up a chair beside her hospital bed

and sat down. Too many years had gone by since he'd seen Miss Annabel, and as he gazed at her care-worn face, the passage of time became almost painful. Her hair had gone completely white, and her skin had that fragile, paper-thin quality that came with age and pain.

She'd seemed a little melancholic when Nathan first arrived, but her spirits had improved with his gift. Pearls had always been her passion.

"This is one of the last pearls I found before I left Arcadia years ago," he explained. "I'd be honored if you'd consider adding it to your private collection."

"Bless your heart. I'm the one who's honored." She reached over and patted Nathan's hand. "You've always been a favorite of mine, but then, I suspect you already know that, don't you?"

Nathan felt a sudden stab of guilt for not having come to visit her sooner. And for coming here now under false pretenses.

"So how are things at the paper? Virgil driving you crazy?" she asked, with the same uncanny insight Nathan remembered too well.

He'd never been able to lie to Miss Annabel and get away with it, so he didn't even try. "It's been an adjustment, to say the least," he said with a sigh. "But Virgil isn't the only problem. The *Argus* is going through some tough times."

"Even more reason you should keep this pearl." She tried to hand it back to Nathan, but he curled his fingers over hers.

"No way. I've wanted to give you that pearl for a long time, and besides, it's value is mostly sentimental. It may be pretty, but it doesn't compare to the gems you have in your shop.''

''It's beautiful, Nathan, and I'll treasure it always.'' Annabel's eyes glinted suspiciously for a moment, but she blinked back her tears with the same stoicism he'd seen in Shelby. ''As for the *Argus,* the shop has a running ad every Sunday and a full-page at least once a month. You can tell Virgil he can count on that to continue.''

''I appreciate that.'' Nathan paused now that she'd given him the perfect opening. ''Actually, that's one of the reasons I came to see you. How would you feel about a little free publicity for the Pearl Cove?''

Annabel's blue eyes—so like Shelby's—lit with interest. ''I'm listening.''

''I'd like to do a piece on Shelby, her return to Arcadia and her management of the shop during your recuperation. That sort of thing.'' He gauged Annabel's reaction carefully as he spoke. ''How do you think she'd feel about it?''

A shadow flickered across Annabel's face. ''This wasn't your idea, was it?''

Nathan shrugged. ''Virgil suggested it, and truthfully, I didn't care much for it at first. But I think he's right, Miss Annabel. Shelby's return to Arcadia is newsworthy.''

''That's all you plan to write about? Her running the shop for me? Nothing about her past?''

''To do the story justice, it would have to be an in-depth piece,'' Nathan explained reluctantly. ''Shelby survived something few of us will ever have to go through, and she seems to be even stronger for it. It's a good angle.''

Annabel gazed at him sadly. "But it was such a terrible time for her, Nathan. I don't think you realize. No one should have to go through what Shelby did. It wasn't bad enough that she lost her husband to that madman, but then he came after her. He very nearly destroyed her, and even now…how do you think she feels, with her husband dead and that animal still alive? How do you think she sleeps at night, knowing that if he ever got out of prison, he might come after her again?"

The thought of Lunt anywhere near Shelby brought Nathan's protective instincts roaring out of hibernation. "That's not going to happen. Not if I have anything to say about it."

Annabel's gaze softened. "You were always so very protective of her. I never spent a moment worrying about Shelby when I knew she was with you."

Nathan thought it was the highest compliment he'd ever been paid, but he wasn't so certain he deserved it. Wasn't he here contemplating a story that he knew Shelby would object to? Wasn't he considering exploiting her pain for the sake of redeeming not just the *Argus* but his own reputation as a journalist? If the paper failed, so did he. He couldn't let that happen.

Annabel squeezed his hand. "I'm not going to advise you one way or another about that story because I know, regardless of what I say, you'll do the right thing where Shelby's concerned."

"I think you give me too much credit. I don't want to hurt Shelby, but I also have a responsibility to my readers. People still haven't forgotten what happened to her when she was a kid. The way she became a celebrity. They're still curious about her.''

"You mean the monster sighting." Annabel's gaze dropped to the pearl she still held in her palm. "I've always wondered about that night myself," she murmured.

"What do you mean?"

She gave him a shrewd look. "Off the record?"

He nodded.

"Shelby wasn't the type of child to make up stories. I've always been convinced she saw something that night. Whether or not it was the Pearl River Monster, I couldn't say. But she did see something.''

"What's your best guess?"

Her expression grew troubled. "I don't know. I've never been one to believe in the supernatural, but when you've lived on the river as long as I have, you come to appreciate that some things can't be explained. Plenty of times I've been spooked for no good reason.''

"And yet you've stayed out there all these years," Nathan said. "Didn't you ever consider moving into town?"

"Not once," she said almost defiantly. "My husband built that house for me after he came home from the war. I wouldn't dream of moving. Besides, I'm just an old river rat at heart. It'd take more than the Pearl River Monster to scare me away from my home." This last was said with a spark of humor in her eyes, and Nathan grinned.

"I don't know, Miss Annabel. A two-hundred pound loggerhead might do it for me.''

She gave a cackle of delighted laughter. "I swear,

you're a sight for sore eyes, Nathan. I'm glad you came to see me today.''

"So am I.''

"But I suspect,'' she said with that dreaded intuition, "You've yet to tell me the real reason for your visit.''

Nathan frowned. "What are you talking about? I wanted to bring you the pearl and to ask your opinion about doing a story on Shelby.''

She lifted a brow. "I believe what you really came to ask me about was Shelby's husband.''

Nathan's first instinct was to deny it, but what would be the use? She'd see right through him. "Okay,'' he said with a shrug. "So tell me what he was like.''

She sighed. "Michael was a good man. Kind. Decent. Very successful. And he doted on Shelby. Thought the sun rose and set on her. I believe he would have done anything for her. But...''

"But?'' Nathan prompted, when she left her sentence dangling.

"But he wasn't the right man for my Shelby.''

Nathan's heart gave a sharp rap against his chest, as if to make sure he was paying attention. "Why not?'' he tried to ask calmly.

"Don't get me wrong. Shelby loved Michael. If he'd lived, I think their marriage would have lasted. I think she would have been reasonably happy. But reasonably happy isn't enough in my book. Life's too short.''

Was that why his mother had left? Nathan wondered suddenly. Had she only been "reasonably happy'' with Nathan and his father? Had that not been enough for her, either?

Nathan hadn't thought about his mother in years, but since his conversation with Shelby the night before, he couldn't seem to get her off his mind. His mother…or Shelby.

He glanced up to find Annabel's pensive gaze on him. "All those years that you and Shelby were as thick as thieves, I kept waiting for your friendship to blossom into something more, something deeper. It was so obvious to me that you two were meant for each other, and yet, neither one of you could see it."

You're wrong, Nathan thought. He'd been crazy about Shelby from the moment he'd first laid eyes on her.

Annabel chuckled ruefully. "Considering how much time the two of you spent together, I suppose I should be grateful you *didn't* see what I saw. Especially after you became teenagers."

"Maybe you were imagining things," Nathan said. "You always were a romantic."

"It's not too late." Annabel took his hand between both of hers and held it warmly. "But Shelby won't make it easy for you. She feels guilty for Michael's death, and that will make it even more difficult for her to let go. She'll see you as a threat. She'll use any excuse not to be with you. But make no mistake about it, Nathan. She needs you. No matter what she says or does to the contrary, she needs you in her life."

"Maybe we should let Shelby decide that."

"Decide what?" a voice demanded from the doorway.

Chapter Seven

"Why, Shelby!" her grandmother said in surprise. "I didn't know you were coming by to see me after work today. How's the shop?"

"Just fine. How are you feeling, Grandmother?"

"Much better, now that you and Nathan are here."

The way she linked their names made Shelby think of the dream again. Almost against her will, her gaze went to Nathan's, and she could feel her cheeks start to heat.

Something glinted in his dark eyes, and Shelby had the mortifying notion that he could tell what she was thinking. That he knew about her dream. That it was entirely too likely he'd had the same one.

"My goodness, but you're warm," Annabel remarked worriedly as Shelby bent down to kiss her cheek. "You're not coming down with something, are you?" She tried to check Shelby's forehead, but Shelby quickly stepped back out of her reach.

"It's hot outside," she mumbled. "So what is it I'm supposed to decide about?"

Annabel's eyes narrowed with curiosity as she appraised first Shelby, then Nathan. Her grandmother had always been just a little too astute for Shelby's peace of mind.

"As a matter of fact, Nathan was just asking me about—"

"—Takamura Industries," he cut in. "I wanted to find out how well your grandmother knows Yoshi Takamura."

Annabel's eyes gleamed with sudden amusement. "I guess we were just getting to that part."

Shelby frowned. "I don't understand. What does Takamura have to do with me?"

Nathan looked momentarily at a loss, but Annabel said smoothly, "Remember, I told you he's been trying to buy the Tubb collection. I've turned him down, of course, but he's been very persistent. You may have to deal with him at some point."

"Why do you think he wants those pearls so badly?" Nathan asked.

Annabel shrugged. "Who knows? You would think he's taken enough from the river, but I guess he still wants more."

"Have you heard anything about the experiments he's allegedly conducting at his lab?" Nathan addressed the question to Annabel, but his gaze was back on Shelby.

"Oh, there's been talk, and if you believe everything you hear, we may soon have a bunch of three-headed toads hopping all over the place." She gave a little laugh, but her expression sobered almost at once. "Seriously, I don't know what he's up to, but I can tell you this. Meddling with nature is a tricky business. If Yoshi's not careful, he's apt to destroy what little mussel population there is left in the river.

But then, why would he care? He's made his millions."

Yoshi? Since when had her grandmother been on a first-name basis with Takamura? Shelby had been under the impression they were only passing acquaintances.

And her attitude. That was another thing that puzzled Shelby. Her grandmother made her living selling pearls taken from the river, and yet she seemed to have nothing but contempt for Takamura, who had done virtually the same with shelling.

Her grandmother had always been scrupulously fair. If she bore a grudge against Yoshi Takamura, then Shelby knew she must have a very good reason for doing so. But Shelby couldn't help wondering what that reason might be.

"So I guess that means you haven't sold Takamura *any* of the pearls from the Tubb collection," she said.

"Of course not," her grandmother said sharply.

So where had those missing pearls gone to? Shelby worried. Was it possible someone else was selling the collection to Takamura, a few pearls at a time? Who had access to the vault? James? Delfina?

"Look, you two obviously have business to discuss," Nathan said. "I'd better shove off."

"You don't have to hurry off on my account." But a part of Shelby hoped he would. The way he kept looking at her—all that intensity—was more than a bit disconcerting. She couldn't help but compare it to the way he'd looked at her in her dream.

You're so beautiful, Shelby. I want to...

"Shelby?"

She roused herself at once. Both her grandmother and Nathan were gazing at her inquiringly. "Yes?"

"Where did you go off to just now?" Annabel was looking amused again.

Shelby felt her face color. "I was just thinking about the shop. There's something I need to discuss with you."

"As I was telling your grandmother, I'd be happy to give you a ride back to Arcadia," Nathan said.

"What?" She stared at him in confusion. "But I don't need a ride. I brought my own car."

"It's a rental," Annabel pointed out. "I don't see any profit in wasting good money when I have a car sitting at home in the garage. You can turn in the rental and catch a ride home with Nathan. My keys are where they always were."

Shelby had to admit it was a sensible idea, but under the circumstances, she wasn't so certain she wanted to be owing any favors to Nathan. Much less to be alone with him for the hour it would take to get home. "But I just got here," she protested. "There's something I need to talk to you about."

"No problem." Nathan had stood when Shelby came into the room and now he headed toward the door. "I have an appointment at the crime lab. Why don't I meet you back here in, say, an hour?" He glanced at his watch. "Will that give you enough time?"

No way out of it now, Shelby thought in alarm. Still, her grandmother was right. Having a rental car was a waste of money, and there was no good reason why she shouldn't ride home with Nathan.

No good reason except for that pesky little dream she'd had last night.

She glanced at him and shrugged. "If you're sure it won't be an inconvenience."

"None at all. I'd be glad for the company." He turned to her grandmother. "It was nice visiting with you, Miss Annabel."

She gave him a brilliant smile. "Don't be such a stranger, Nathan, you hear me? And don't forget what we discussed."

"I won't." His gaze brushed Shelby again before he turned to leave.

She felt a tremble of excitement in her stomach as she watched him disappear through the door. Sensible or not, riding home with Nathan wasn't a good idea. Too many things had happened to rattle her since she'd awakened that morning, and at the moment, she felt a little too shaky to deal with her attraction for him.

She turned to Annabel anxiously. "What was he really doing here, Grandmother?"

Her grandmother lifted her brows in surprise. "Why, Shelby Kay August. If I didn't know better, I'd say you sound suspicious of Nathan's motives. Why shouldn't he come here to see me? He's always been like a grandson to me. See what he brought me?" She held out her hand so that Shelby could examine the pearl.

"It's lovely."

"Isn't it? That boy always did have an eye for quality." Her grandmother's smile was guileless, but Shelby wasn't fooled.

"Grandmother," she warned. "Why are you talking up Nathan to me, all of a sudden? You're not trying to matchmake, I hope.''

"Shelby!'' Her grandmother tried to draw herself up indignantly, but her injury hampered her effort and she winced. "Do you really think I'd be that insensitive? I know what you've been through since Michael died.''

"Well, it just seemed as if—''

"After all, I know what it's like to lose a husband.'' Annabel plucked at an invisible thread on the front of her pale yellow bed jacket. "I would never have dreamed of seeing another man after your grandfather died. It would have been disloyal to Henry if I'd fallen in love with someone else. A betrayal of the worst sort. No.'' She gave Shelby a piercing glance. "It was far better that I spent these last thirty years alone.''

"All right, your point is taken.'' Shelby gave her grandmother an annoyed look. "But I'm not ready to move on, Grandmother. It's hardly been more than a year.''

"I know that.'' Her grandmother suddenly looked very old and indescribably sad as she gazed up at Shelby. "But sometimes fate just has plain bad timing, Shelby. A year or five years. Or thirty years, for that matter. What difference does it make? Michael is gone, but you have the rest of your life. Don't live it in the past, as I did. Michael wouldn't want that.''

Shelby glanced down, hiding her sudden tears from her grandmother. "I don't want to forget him.''

"Who says you have to forget him? He'll always be right here with you.'' She leaned over and touched her aged hand to Shelby's heart. "No one will ever take his place. But there's room in your heart for both of them, child.''

"Both of them?"

Annabel smiled. "Whoever you might someday fall in love with."

"And you want that person to be Nathan," Shelby accused.

"Did I say that?"

"You didn't have to. I can read you like a book, Grandmother."

Annabel sighed. "I must be losing my touch then. I hate getting old."

"You're not getting old. You're just getting a little transparent."

"Just as bad," Annabel grumbled. She gazed up at Shelby. "He's a good man, Shelby."

"I know that."

"I won't deny he's made his share of mistakes. Bad ones. All that business in Washington." Her grandmother's eyes clouded for a moment.

"What business in Washington?" Shelby asked curiously.

Annabel shrugged. "It's not my place to say. I expect Nathan will tell you himself in due time. But just remember, Shelby, that no one is perfect. And in spite of everything, I believe Nathan's heart has always been in the right place."

Shelby believed that, too. But she hadn't come here to talk about Nathan, and she didn't think it a good idea to encourage her grandmother's hopes. There was never going to be anything more than friendship between Shelby and Nathan, and the sooner Annabel accepted that, the better.

"Grandmother, I really didn't come here to talk to you about Nathan. I want to talk to you about the Tubb collection."

Disappointment—or was it annoyance?—flickered across her grandmother's features. "What about it?"

"You said you haven't sold any loose pearls to Takamura, but have you had any other recent sales?"

Annabel frowned. "No. Why?"

"I've been through the containers in the vault," Shelby explained. "According to the inventory sheets, we're missing some pearls. Do you have any out on consignment with other dealers that haven't been entered into the computer?"

"No." Her grandmother looked worried now. "The inventory sheets should be accurate. Delfina and I updated them just last month. Are you sure your tally was accurate?"

"I counted twice," Shelby said. "But it's possible I missed some. I'll recheck when I go in to work in the morning, but in the meantime, does Delfina have access to the vault? Or...anyone else?"

Their gazes met, and Shelby knew her grandmother was thinking, as she was, of James. Annabel shook her head. "You're the only one I've given the combination to, but I'll admit, I haven't always been as diligent as I should have been about locking up. I suppose it's possible someone could have gotten to the pearls while I was busy."

Shelby thought of Delfina and James letting themselves into the shop. They both had keys. Either of them could come and go as they pleased.

She also remembered that James had said yesterday about his mother's state of mind. But being a little absentminded or careless didn't make one incompetent.

Still, Shelby silently vowed to keep a closer eye on things herself from now on.

"I'm sure it's nothing to be concerned about." She forced an optimism in her tone she was far from feeling. "I was a little distracted this morning, so I probably counted wrong, that's all. I don't want you worrying about this."

"I'm sure you're right," Annabel agreed, but her gaze remained troubled. "Don't say anything about this to anyone else. Not yet. Delfina is not at all a materialistic or greedy person. I can't imagine her stealing from me, but if she did take the pearls, then she must have had a desperate reason for doing so. I wouldn't want her to get in any trouble with the law. And if it was James..." She trailed off, drawing a long, weary breath. "I'd rather think it was a stranger."

"I know."

"But regardless of who the culprit turns out to be—" Annabel reached out and clutched Shelby's hand. "You be careful. I'd hate to think I've put you in danger by asking you to come back home."

"I'll be fine, Grandmother. Don't worry about me."

But Shelby had a sudden vision of the shadow she'd glimpsed down by the river last night. Did that shadow have anything to do with the missing pearls?

She couldn't help thinking that her uncle James was behind it all. Had he been skulking down by the river last night to try and frighten her? Or was his purpose more dire than that? More dangerous.

...if you think I'm going to let you waltz in here and take what's rightfully mine, you're in for a very nasty surprise.

A shudder of fear racked Shelby suddenly, but she tried to hide it from her grandmother. She was thinking about the mutilated rabbit now, about the blood trail that had been left for her to find.

Like Lunt, had James left her a grisly warning?

"WHY DON'T YOU go to the police?" Nathan demanded. He gave her a stern glance as he merged right after having passed a long line of slow-moving cars on the interstate.

A logical question, Shelby thought, but the situation was much more complicated than he realized. She wasn't certain why she'd even told him about the missing pearls except that she was more worried than she'd let on to her grandmother. Plus, she thought Nathan might have some idea of what she should do. He did, but unfortunately, going to the police wasn't an option.

With a sigh, Shelby turned to gaze out the window at what seemed like an endless blur of car dealerships that had sprung up on the outskirts of the city. Overhead, a formation of air force jets banked left, heading for their base. Shelby watched them for a moment before turning back to Nathan. "Grandmother asked me not to go to the police. I think she's worried that either Delfina or James took the pearls, and she doesn't want to get them in trouble."

"But this is serious business, Shelby. You can't sit back and let someone rob her blind."

"I don't intend to." She bristled slightly at his

admonishment. "But Grandmother admitted to me that she hasn't been as careful as she should have been about keeping the vault locked. I would imagine that applies to the back door of the shop as well. If I told the police about that, Grandmother might come off looking...forgetful."

"So what?"

"So, James has threatened to go to court to have her declared incompetent."

"What?" Nathan shot her an outraged glance. "That's not an easy thing to prove. What the hell does he plan to claim as grounds?"

Shelby folded her arms in front of her. "Me, for one thing. He doesn't think Grandmother should have put me in charge of the shop because I was—" She broke off abruptly, glancing back out the window. No need to tell Nathan about the nightmares. The sleepwalking. The difficulties she'd had after her attack. "Let's just say, he doesn't seem to have much faith in my abilities. If Grandmother's carelessness becomes a matter of public record, he could use that against her, too."

"I see your point." Nathan paused. "Look, maybe I can help you out here."

"How?"

"I'll snoop around a little, see what I can find out about James's latest business venture. Sounds to me as if he's pretty desperate to get his hands on some cash. If we can find out what he's up to—that he has an ulterior motive for wanting Miss Annabel declared incompetent in order to gain control of her finances—we can probably get any motion he files dismissed."

"You'd do that?" Shelby didn't know why she was so surprised by Nathan's offer. He'd always been willing to lend a helping hand. He was, as her grandmother said, a good man.

"I'll be happy to help any way I can," he said warmly. Their gazes met briefly before Shelby quickly glanced away. But in that moment, she had seen something else gleaming in Nathan's dark eyes. Attraction. Lust. Baser emotions that made her tremble with awareness.

"Actually," he said softly. "There's a favor I'd like to ask of you."

Shelby was almost afraid to ask the nature of his request. But she was more afraid that she might actually be tempted to grant it.

His gaze turned faintly challenging. "Don't you want to know what it is?"

"I'm not sure," she admitted. "I remember the trouble some of your favors used to get me into."

"Yeah, but this time I promise you won't be risking life or limb."

"I've heard that one before," she said dryly.

Come on, Shelby. Let go of the rope. The water's not that deep.

Come on, Shelby. It's just a little ol' garden snake. Nothing to be afraid of.

Come on, Shelby. Meet me down by the river at midnight. They say that's the best time to see the monster.

"So what do you say?" Nathan prompted.

She turned to face him. "Okay, let's hear it," she said grudgingly.

"I need your pearl expertise for the story I'm working on about Takamura Industries."

Shelby lifted a brow. *"My* expertise? You were the pearl diver."

"Yeah, but I was just a kid, and I didn't pay much attention to the business end of shelling. My knowledge of the cultured-pearl industry is limited, to say the least."

"Then why didn't you talk to Grandmother? She's the real expert," Shelby pointed out.

"Normally, I would have, but I think she should expend her energies on getting well." Nathan gave her a disarming grin. "So I guess you'll just have to do."

The teasing quality of his voice lightened Shelby's mood whether she wanted it to or not. "I'm no expert, but I guess I can give it a shot. What is it you want to know?"

He lifted his hand briefly from the steering wheel, gesturing. "Just pretend I don't know anything. If you were trying to give readers a background about the pearling industry, what do you think they should know?"

Shelby thought for a moment. "Well, the most basic information, I guess, is how pearls are formed. A natural pearl occurs when a grain of sand or a parasitic worm gets inside a mollusk's shell accidentally."

He flashed her an amused glance. "Wonder how many women realize they're wearing the remains of parasitic worms around their necks?"

Shelby couldn't help but laugh. "Not too many. Anyway, the mollusk's reaction is to cover the irritant with layers of nacre. A cultured pearl is created when an irritant, or nucleus, which is usually a bead made from freshwater mussel shells, is surgically inserted into the mollusk, along with mantel tissue. The inserted tissue starts to form the nacre, and the bead is covered in the same way a natural irritant would be. The more layers of nacre that are allowed to form, the better quality the pearl."

"That's where Takamura comes in," Nathan said. "He's been a major supplier of mussel shells to the Japanese pearl farms for years. It's a huge business."

Shelby nodded. "The whole pearling industry is big business and has been for centuries. But the culturing process started a revolution."

Nathan gave her a studied glance. "What would you say if I told you I think Takamura may be working on something that could have an equal or greater impact on the pearling industry as the culturing process?"

Shelby perked up with interest. "Like what?"

"I've been reading about some recent experiments in Japan that involve genetic engineering. By keeping mantel tissue from a mollusk alive indefinitely in a test tube, it may be possible for pearls to be produced almost entirely in a laboratory." Again he gestured with his hand. "These are not synthetic pearls, but real cultured pearls, virtually identical to the ones created inside a mollusk. Imagine the advantages of such a process. Lab-created pearls wouldn't be subjected to the same natural disasters that have recently befallen pearl farmers, and with precise genetic engineering, size and quality could also be controlled."

Shelby listened to him intently, eagerly absorbing

everything he told her. She'd been away from the pearl industry for years, but she'd never lost her fascination for what her grandmother always called the most romantic gems. "You think Takamura is conducting his own genetic-engineering experiments using freshwater mussels?"

"It wouldn't surprise me," Nathan said. "But carry those experiments one step further. What if he planned to pass the lab-created pearls off as natural pearls instead of cultured pearls?"

Shelby shook her head. "He'd never get away with that. He'd still have to use a nucleus for the nacre to start forming, and the bead can be detected by X ray."

"What if he found a way to eliminate the nucleus?"

"I don't see how that would ever be possible."

He glanced at her again. "It would be, if the nucleus was created from a gel-like substance that dissolves once the pearl starts forming. Hypothetically speaking, what would be the consequences of such a development?"

Shelby gave him a worried look. "Hypothetically speaking, he could make millions." *Was* this all hypothetical, or had Nathan stumbled onto something diabolical afoot in Takamura's lab? "A natural South Sea pearl can retail thirty or forty times more than a good-quality cultured pearl."

"What about freshwater pearls?"

"Traditionally, they haven't been valued as highly as South Sea pearls, but the price can be quite high—thousands of dollars—for a good-quality, natural freshwater pearl."

"If someone were to suddenly put a quantity of natural pearls on the market, it might look a little suspicious," Nathan mused. "But if it were made known that the pearls had been part of a private collection—"

"Like the Tubb collection?" Shelby stared at him in astonishment. "You think that's why Takamura wants my grandmother's pearls so badly?"

Nathan shrugged. "I think he's an ambitious man, and now that the mussel population in the river is so badly depleted, he'll have to look elsewhere for his fortune."

"But he's already rich. He'd be risking an awful lot on a scheme like this."

"Maybe, maybe not." Another shrug. "Maybe once the process is perfected, his plan is to sell it to the highest bidder. The risk for him would be minimal."

Shelby frowned. "Have you talked to him? Asked him flat out about his lab?"

"I've tried, but I can't get past his secretary."

She lifted a brow. "With your tenacity? That surprises me."

He flashed her an irritated look. "You haven't met his secretary. She looks as if she could...never mind. Let's just say, she's not a woman I'd want to tangle with—in more ways than one."

"I get the picture." The thought of Nathan "tangling" with a woman—in more ways than one— gave Shelby an odd, tight feeling in her chest.

"They're all amazingly tight-lipped around that place." He scowled at the road. "The company hasn't even released an official statement regarding Danny Weathers's death.''

''What does Takamura have to do with Danny's death?''

''Maybe nothing,'' he conceded. ''But Danny worked for Takamura as a diver. You would think, at the very least, he'd release a statement regarding the tragic death of one of his employees.''

They fell silent for a moment, and Shelby noticed they were nearing the Arcadia exit. She was surprised to find how quickly the trip had gone by. Glancing at Nathan almost shyly, she said, ''Thanks for giving me a ride. I guess I didn't sound too appreciative at first.''

''No problem. And besides, you've more than paid for the trip with the information you've given me.''

''Oh, sure. Like you hadn't already done your research.'' Shelby glanced at his profile. ''You don't need me for this story. I'd never even heard of the genetic-engineering experiments, much less a dissolving nucleus. Where did you read about all this stuff anyway?''

''I have my sources.''

''And obviously they're better informed than I am,'' she said dryly.

''I wouldn't say that. Besides, I value your opinion. Which brings me to another favor I need to ask of you.'' Nathan took the exit ramp, and as they rolled toward Arcadia, his expression became almost grim. ''I'd like you to go with me to see Danny's widow.''

Chapter Eight

Nathan was surprised that Shelby so readily agreed to his request, although she'd grown very silent ever since. Her gaze remained glued to the window as they crossed the long bridge over the river that brought them into Arcadia.

Twilight fell slowly this time of year, and the lengthening shadows softened the weathered facade of the once graceful homes lining Riverside Drive. Even with the windows up, Nathan could smell the magnolias, and the scent took him straight back to his boyhood.

Growing up, he'd thought the white, two-story houses along Riverside Drive with their shady front porches and well-tended lawns, were the ultimate in elegance. The social stature between the kids who lived in this area and the ones who grew up on the river was vast, but all that had changed now.

In recent years, the more affluent families had moved to the new subdivisions at the edge of town, and Riverside had hit hard times. The signs of decline were everywhere—the peeling paint, the sagging balconies, the broken-down cars parked along the street—but nowhere more poignantly than in the suspicious eyes of the neighborhood children as Nathan and Shelby drove by. Here, in what once had been an enclave of refined living, kids had been warned to be extremely wary of strangers.

He turned right on LaGrange and headed north, to where several small housing developments had cropped up near the old air base. The homes here were almost indistinguishable from one another, but Nathan had been to Danny's home before. They'd met there a few nights ago and had stood talking on the front yard about old times. And about Takamura Industries.

Two cars were parked in the driveway and another at the curb. Lights shone from the windows in the front of the house, but a forlorn air had settled over the place. Neighbors walking their dogs and watering their yards stopped and watched as Nathan and Shelby got out of the car and headed up the walkway to the house.

"I'm still not sure about this," she said, as they waited for someone to answer the doorbell. Her arms were wrapped around her middle, and she looked very small and vulnerable suddenly, as if she were empathizing a little too closely with Gayla Weathers's bereavement. "I hate to intrude at a time like this."

"It'll be all right." Her empathy was one of the reasons Nathan had wanted her to come with him. Gayla would be more comfortable—and therefore more likely to open up—in the presence of another woman, one who understood what she was going through. The other reason was more basic. Nathan simply wanted Shelby's company.

The door opened and a middle-aged woman wearing a blue-and-white-gingham apron gazed back at them.

"Yes?"

"I'm Nathan Dallas and this is Shelby August. I wonder if we could have a moment with Gayla... Mrs. Weathers."

"I'm Gayla's mother." She wiped her hands on her apron, then pushed back a lock of dark hair from her face. "Nathan Dallas, you say? Are you Virgil's nephew? The one who's working at the *Argus?*"

"Yes, ma'am." Nathan wondered if she might turn them away, knowing that he was connected to the newspaper, but instead, she opened the screen door and stepped out onto the tiny porch.

"We just got today's paper a little while ago. Gayla saw the piece you wrote about Danny." She reached over and placed her hand on Nathan's arm. "I can't thank you enough. You don't know how much reading those nice things about Danny has helped her."

"I'm glad." Nathan was unaccountably touched by the woman's words. The piece he'd done on Danny wasn't his usual sort of writing. The article contained none of his suspicions concerning Danny's death, no in-depth investigation of the circumstances, no hard-edge reporting of the facts. Instead, Nathan had reminisced about their boyhood friendship, recalling the times they'd camped out on Cypress Island together, the stories they'd shared over a campfire, their exploration of the river in a homemade canoe.

Nathan wasn't certain what had possessed him to write such a piece—guilt, perhaps, for having used their friendship to get information about Takamura—but he was glad now that he had.

"Gayla's inside," her mother told them warmly. "Come on in. I'm sure she'd like to see you." She glanced at Shelby and smiled. "You're Miss Annabel's granddaughter, aren't you? I remember you because I always liked the name *Shelby*."

"Thank you." Shelby extended her hand to the woman. "I'm sorry if we're intruding, Mrs....?"

"Spivey. But please call me June," she said, taking Shelby's hand. She turned then and led them inside, saying over her shoulder, "I heard about your grandmother's accident. How is she doing?"

"She's on the mend," Shelby said. "But it'll take a while."

"The older we get, the longer it takes." The woman ushered them through a tiny, spotless living room and dining area into the kitchen at the back of the house.

A younger version of Mrs. Spivey sat at a small wooden table surveying with what looked like dismay the dozens of covered casserole dishes lining every square inch of counter space in the kitchen.

She must have heard them come in because she made a helpless gesture toward the dishes, but she didn't look up. "I don't know what we're going to do with all this food, Mama."

"You let me worry about that, sweetie. I'll take care of everything. Look who's come to see you."

Gayla turned, her puzzled gaze going from Nathan to Shelby. Her fingers toyed with the top button on her black dress. "I don't—Nathan?"

"I wasn't certain you'd remember me." He'd met her briefly when he'd come by to see Danny the other night. Although he knew Gayla'd grown up in Arcadia, he had only a vague recollection of her as a kid, probably because she was several years younger.

Tragically young for a widow, he thought, his gaze moving to Shelby once more. "This is Shelby August," he said, putting his hand on her elbow.

"Miss Annabel's granddaughter," Mrs. Spivey supplied.

"Oh. *Oh!*" Gayla's weary gaze lit in recognition. "You're the one who saw the Pearl River Monster that time!"

Nathan felt Shelby stiffen, but her voice was only slightly hesitant when she spoke. "That was a long time ago."

Gayla nodded. "I know. I don't remember much about those days. I was only three or four at the time, but Danny talked about it once in a while. He always believed you. He never thought you'd made that story up, like some of the others around here did."

Shelby seemed at a loss for a moment. "That's... nice to know."

Gayla nodded vaguely. "He loved the river, you know. He was around it all his life, but if I heard him say once, I heard him say a thousand times, 'Gayla, there's something in that river. Something that doesn't belong there. I'd stake my life Shelby Westmoreland was telling the truth about what she saw that night.'"

"Did he ever...see it?" Shelby's voice sounded tentative, as if she were almost afraid of Gayla's answer.

But the woman shook her head. "No, he never claimed he saw it. It was more like a feeling he got when he was diving, he said. Like something was watching him. A presence, he called it."

"Did he say he'd had that feeling recently?" Nathan pressed.

Gayla glanced up at him and nodded. "He said it just a few nights ago."

"My goodness gracious," Mrs. Spivey said a little too brightly. "All this talk about monsters. I never heard of such nonsense. Why don't I fix us all a cup of coffee?"

"No, thank you." Shelby glanced at Nathan. "We can't stay long."

He nodded in agreement. "We just came by to pay our respects to your family."

"Well, I'll go see about the children while y'all have a visit." June Spivey glanced at her daughter worriedly. "Leave all this food, Gayla, honey, you hear me? I'll take care of it later. You need to get some rest."

"I will, Mama." After her mother left, Gayla motioned for Nathan and Shelby to sit with her at the table. "Mama showed me what you wrote about Danny in the paper," she said quietly. "It was beautiful. I had her go out and buy extra copies. I'm going to frame one for each of the kids so when they're older, they'll remember what you wrote about their daddy."

Nathan didn't know what to say to that. He

glanced at Shelby, but it was hard to tell what she was thinking. The visit was bound to be stirring some terrible memories for her, but she seemed to be handling it well.

"I know this is a difficult time for you," he said to Gayla. "But I wonder if I could ask you some questions about Danny's diving."

She remained silent for a moment, gazing down at her hands. Finally she said softly, "The sheriff says it was an accident, but Danny knew that river like the back of his hand. It's hard for me to believe he could have been so careless."

"You don't believe his death was accidental?"

She lifted her gaze. "Do you?"

"I saw the autopsy report," Nathan said gently. "It bears out the sheriff's conclusion."

"That still doesn't explain who was out there in that boat that night," she said angrily. "Or why they didn't try to help Danny once they'd hit him. Why didn't they go for help? If it was an accident, why hasn't anyone come forward?"

Nathan didn't bother giving her all the logical arguments, because he didn't believe them himself. "Did Danny go night-diving a lot?"

"Here lately he did. He said it didn't matter if it was night or day because the river's so murky, it's like being in a cave anyway. Once you're down there, you can't see much of anything."

Nathan remembered that terrible feeling of blindness, of not being able to do much more than feel your way along the bottom. And the currents could play havoc with your senses. "Was he diving for shells?"

Again Gayla hesitated, her expression suddenly wary. "I guess it won't matter if I tell you now. He had a secret spot where he'd found a lot of shells, but he didn't want word to get out. He wouldn't even tell me where it was. But he did say he'd already found several pearls in some of the mussels, good ones, and that's very unusual. Sometimes you can go through two- or three-hundred shells without finding even a seed pearl. He'd been selling them to Miss Annabel..." She trailed off, glancing at Shelby. "But he didn't worry about her, because he said Miss Annabel knew how it was with pearl divers. She knew how to keep their secrets."

"Did Danny's employer know about the spot?" Nathan asked.

"Takamura?" Something flickered in Gayla's eyes, an emotion that might have been fear. She cast her gaze downward, staring at the picture of Danny on the front page of the *Argus*. "I don't think so."

"Did Danny ever talk about the lab? About Takamura's experiments?"

"I don't know anything about Takamura." There was no mistaking Gayla's fear now. Quickly, she rose from the table, dabbing at her eyes with a lace hankie. "I'm sorry. I don't think I can talk about this anymore. Will you excuse me?"

She fled from the room in what seemed to Nathan near panic.

"THANKS FOR GOING over there with me." He pulled into Shelby's driveway and parked.

"I owed you," she said with a shrug, glancing out the window. "But we're even now." It was seriously dark by this time, and Shelby shivered as she gazed at her grandmother's house. She hated coming home at night.

As if sensing her trepidation, Nathan opened his door. "Let me walk you to the porch. It's pretty dark tonight."

She didn't turn him down. It was easy to get spooked out here, and ever since their conversation with Gayla Weathers, Shelby had been feeling a little edgy. She wasn't certain if the talk about her monster sighting had caused her uneasiness, or if it had been the look of fear in Gayla's eyes when Nathan had mentioned Takamura.

The laboratory wasn't all that far from here. What if Takamura really was conducting strange experiments?

What if his experiments had produced a creature straight from the frames of a B horror movie? Something that mutilated sweet little rabbits and climbed trellises?

You're losing it but good this time, Shelby admonished herself as they mounted the porch steps. But she couldn't help glancing down at the space beneath the house. She fervently hoped nothing lurked in the dampness other than perhaps a new litter of kittens. Tomorrow she might even get up enough courage to go looking for them.

"So what did you make of everything Gayla told us?" she asked Nathan. They were on the porch now, and he stood leaning against one of the white posts, gazing off toward the river. Shelby moved to the railing beside him.

"I'm trying to figure out how it ties in with what

we talked about earlier.'' Nathan frowned at the water. ''I keep wondering about those pearls she said Danny found recently. What if they had something to do with Takamura?''

''Like how?''

''What if they were lab-produced and Danny only claimed he'd found them in the river?''

''You mean you think he may have stolen them?''

Nathan shrugged. ''There haven't been many pearls in this river for a long time. Then suddenly, Danny finds such a productive spot. You have to admit, it's curious, to say the least.''

''I guess if we knew precisely where this 'secret spot' was located, you could check it out for yourself,'' Shelby suggested, only half-serious.

''Oh, I know where it is.'' Nathan turned to stare down at her. The light Shelby had left on earlier filtered softly through the lace curtains, creating just enough illumination to give her a glimpse of his features. His eyes were like obsidian pools. Deep and fathomless. Dangerous, if you weren't careful.

''How do you know?''

''Because I followed him one night.''

''Why?''

Nathan glanced back at the river. ''We reporters have our secrets, too, but since you've agreed to help me out with this story…''

''Wait a minute,'' she cut in sharply. ''I never agreed to help you.''

''Sure you did.'' He sounded a little amused. ''You're my pearl expert, remember?''

''I've already told you everything I know,''

Shelby protested. ''Which is not nearly as much as you seem to.''

''Come on, Shelby. Now you're being modest,'' he teased. ''You were always like a sponge around your grandmother. You had a passion for pearls every bit the equal of hers. I'm surprised you didn't come back here before now to help her with the business.''

''I was married,'' she reminded him. ''I had a life in California.''

''Yes,'' he said softly. ''Somehow I keep forgetting about that.''

His gaze was on her again, and the intensity of his stare, the way he looked at her caused a tremor in Shelby's stomach. Made her remember the dream she'd been trying all day to forget.

He reached out a hand to touch her hair.

''Don't do something we'll both regret,'' she warned. But she didn't move away from his touch. She closed her eyes instead, feeling more alone than she ever had before. Missing Michael so much she ached, except...

It wasn't Michael she suddenly longed for. It was Nathan.

''I can't do this.'' She hadn't meant to speak the words aloud, but there they suddenly were, hanging in the air between them.

''I would never ask you to do anything you didn't really want to.'' Nathan wove his fingers in her hair, applying a gentle pressure until she moved toward him. Until they were standing only inches apart. He was so tall, she had to look up at him, and when she tilted her head back, he lowered his mouth to hers.

Her first reaction was to shove him away. Scream in protest. Let him know that she was not his for the taking.

Instead, she stood perfectly still, allowing his lips to whisper over hers in a kiss that held more promise than passion. It was the first time he'd ever kissed her, and Shelby felt a little stunned that it was finally happening. She didn't respond, but she didn't reject him, either.

When he lifted his head, it was to smile down at her. "That wasn't so bad, was it?"

"It wasn't what I expected."

He gave a low, surprised laugh. "I can't let that one pass. Just exactly what were you expecting?"

He'd been more forceful in her dream. Intense, yet tender. Passionate, yet gentle. The perfect lover.

"I'm not sure," she said, embarrassed now.

"Then let's try it again." His gaze deepened in the moonlight. "It seems only fair to give me another shot now that I know I'm working with expectations. I've always been able to perform well under pressure."

Shelby didn't doubt that for a moment, but she wasn't so certain about herself. If she wasn't careful, she just might find herself kissing him back.

"I don't think that would be a good idea." She didn't physically move away from him, but she turned to stare at the river, putting distance between them just the same.

Beside her, Nathan said, "You can't grieve forever, Shelby. You're a young woman. You have your whole life ahead of you."

"There's no timetable for my grief," she said angrily. "And age has nothing to do with it. You can't know what I'm feeling, so please don't presume to."

"I didn't mean to do that." His voice was soft and low, still very intimate. "You're right. I don't know what you're feeling. But I do know what it's like to lose someone you love."

Shelby's anger faded almost immediately. "You mean your mother?"

"Uh, yeah."

"I can't believe you've never tried to find her."

"I explained all that last night."

"I know, but she might still be alive, Nathan. It's not too late."

"It seems I've been hearing that a lot lately," he murmured. He paused, then said, "Did you know she used to work at the *Argus?*"

"What did she do?"

"She wrote a weekly column. I'd forgotten about it myself, but I ran across some of her old bylines the other day when I was looking through the morgue. She was good."

"Maybe you inherited her talent." Shelby turned, studying his profile in the faint light. "Maybe your mother is the reason you became a reporter."

Nathan shrugged. "I never gave it much thought one way or another. It was just something I always wanted to do. The first time I walked into the pressroom at the *Argus* and smelled the ink and the paper, I knew it was in my blood. I never considered doing anything else."

"So why did you come back to Arcadia? Why the *Argus?* You always had such lofty ambitions, and from what I heard, you were well on your way. What happened, Nathan?'' What was "all that business in Washington'' her grandmother had mentioned?

"What makes you think anything happened?'' he asked a little too sharply.

"I'm sorry. I didn't mean to pry—''

"You're right, of course,'' he said bitterly. "Something did happen, but I don't think now is the time to go into it. Let's just say I screwed up royally and leave it at that. I made a lot of bad mistakes, used poor judgment, and my career was over by the time I hit thirty. Everything I'd worked for...'' He ran his hand through his hair and glanced away, as if no longer able to meet Shelby's gaze. "The *Argus* is my last shot. If it doesn't work out, there's nowhere left for me to go.''

Shelby couldn't believe his prospects were as dire as all that. She couldn't believe Nathan had done anything as grim as his expression seemed to suggest. There had never been any doubt in her mind about his integrity, but it had been a long time since she'd known him. Could he have changed that much? It made her sad to think so.

"Look, Shelby, there's something I've been meaning to talk to you about. It's about the *Argus*.'' He straightened from the railing and shoved his hands into his pockets. He gazed down at her with the air of a man about to broach a subject he wasn't too keen on.

"What is it?''

"Remember I told you that I'd recently found some of my mother's old bylines? The reason I was going through the morgue was to find the articles my uncle wrote about you. About your monster sighting."

A prickle of nerves danced along her backbone. *"Why?"*

"How would you feel about letting me interview you for the *Argus*?"

She stared at him in shock. "You're not serious."

"Very serious."

"What would you write about?"

He hesitated. "For starters, what you saw that night down by the river."

Panic bubbled inside Shelby. "That was twenty years ago. I barely remember it."

"But you do have some memory of it," he persisted. "I have a feeling it's shaped your life in ways you may not even realize. Everything that's happened to you since—"

"No," she said coldly. "I won't talk about what happened to Michael. Or to me. I don't want to talk about that night by the river, either. Maybe you've forgotten what happened after the *Argus* printed my uncle's claim, but I became an outcast in this town. A laughingstock."

His gaze flickered in the moonlight. "I'm giving you a chance to set the record straight."

Shelby couldn't believe what he was asking of her. She remembered how tenacious his uncle Virgil had been, how flattered she'd been at first by the attention because she'd been a lonely, confused little girl who'd been abandoned by her parents. But she'd learned her lesson well back then. The press could turn on you just as easily as they could glorify you.

When the media had picked up the story about

Albert Lunt, Shelby had tried to keep her distance. She'd hidden for days on end inside her house, but the reporters had been like a pack of hungry wolves. The moment she emerged from her home, they pounced.

And Lunt's trial...dear God, what a nightmare that had been. The microphones thrust in her face, the probing questions.

To keep her sanity, Shelby had had to remind herself over and over that the reporters were just doing their job. It wasn't personal.

But this *was* personal. This was Nathan, and she couldn't help feeling betrayed.

"Is that what all this has been leading up to?" she asked quietly. "Dinner last night. All the pearl questions today. You wanting to be my friend. You were just trying to draw me in, when all along what you really wanted to do was use me."

"You're taking this the wrong way," he protested. But Shelby noticed he didn't deny her charge.

And the kiss? Was that to soften her resistance as well?

The scary part was, it had almost worked. Shelby had wanted to respond to his kiss. She'd been drawn to his warmth and tenderness in ways she would never have dreamed possible. She'd had to fight her impulses in order to keep her defenses intact, so maybe it was a good thing the truth had come out. Maybe it was a good thing she'd learned Nathan's true motives when she had.

He was willing to betray their friendship for the sake of a story, and that hurt Shelby more deeply than she would have ever imagined. Even in the years they'd been apart, she'd always known in the back of her mind, that she still had Nathan's friendship. That she could always count on him.

Now that had been taken from her, too.

She lifted her chin and gazed up at him. "Look, I understand you have a job to do. I understand this isn't personal for you. But it is for me. I don't want my life made public for your readers' amusement."

"It wouldn't be like that. I would never do anything to exploit your tragedy." Nathan put out a hand toward her, but she stepped back from him instantly. An emotion she couldn't quite define flashed across his face. "If you could just trust me—"

She gazed up at him. "The sad thing is, I did trust you."

"Shelby—"

"I think you'd better go, Nathan."

He looked as if he wanted to argue further, but then he shrugged and moved toward the steps. At the bottom, he turned to stare up at her. "You *can* still trust me, Shelby. Whether you believe me or not, it's the truth."

The truth or not, Shelby couldn't afford to believe it. She'd lost too much already. Putting her trust— and her heart—at risk was not an option she was willing to explore.

IT WAS LATE. The night should have been steeped in silence, but a strange sound had harried Shelby from her restless sleep. She lay very still, listening to the uneven cadence of her own breathing as she tried to decipher the source of her distress. What exactly had she heard? A door closing? Floorboards creaking?

The house was quiet now, and Shelby tried to tell herself she'd imagined the sound. Or dreamed it. But Miss Scarlett lay at the foot of the bed, and in the moonlight streaming in through the window, Shelby could see the fur raised on the cat's back. Her green eyes were wide and softly glowing as she stared at the bedroom door.

Shelby had left the door open when she came to bed, and a lamp illuminated the hallway beyond. For a long, tense moment, she stared into the corridor, watching for the flicker of light, the telltale creep of a shadow, but nothing moved. She could almost convince herself that the sound *had* been her imagination if not for Miss Scarlett's reaction. The cat was clearly alarmed.

"You give new meaning to the term *fraidy cat*," Shelby whispered, but no sooner had the words left her mouth than she heard the sound once more, so softly she wondered how it had awakened her in the first place.

She didn't think it came from within the house, but somewhere close by. The wind blowing a loose shutter? But the trees outside her bedroom window appeared motionless. Not even so much as a leaf fluttered in a stray breeze.

The noise came again, but this time Shelby recognized two distinct sounds. A bump and then a rustle, as if something were being dragged across an uneven floor. Thump, scrape. Thump, scrape.

Her heart pounding even harder, Shelby swung her legs over the bed, feeling for her slippers. Miss Scarlett hadn't moved so much as a whisker until that point, but suddenly she leaped from the bed and scurried underneath, burrowing herself deep in the shadows as if she sensed imminent danger.

The cat's actions were not at all reassuring.

Picking up a heavy flashlight she'd placed on the nightstand, Shelby moved across the floor to the doorway. To do so took tremendous courage. Just a few short weeks ago, she might have buried herself under the covers, terrified and shaking, until morning. A few months ago, she would have called, even in the middle of the night, Dr. Minger for moral support or Detective Hagler for assurances that Lunt couldn't get to her.

A year ago, she might have been taken back to the hospital.

Now, as tempted as she was to scamper under the bed behind Miss Scarlett, Shelby gripped the flashlight and moved into the hallway. She would not live the rest of her life cowering in fear. She would not let herself become Lunt's prisoner.

Besides, Dr. Minger and Detective Hagler were back in L.A. They couldn't help her now. And the last thing Shelby wanted was to call the local authorities. Sheriff McCaid would undoubtedly remember her as the little girl who had caused such a furor by claiming she'd seen a monster. Even if he could suspend his disbelief long enough to send someone to check things out, they might find nothing more than a stray dog chasing a raccoon. Shelby would look ridiculous, and when the incident got out—as it was bound to in such a small town—it might actually give legs to James's claim that she wasn't mentally fit to be in charge of her grandmother's shop. If he brought suit, her grandmother would be devastated.

And Nathan? Well, he'd have a new angle for his story, she thought bitterly.

She could see the moon from the window at the end of the hallway. Even if the lamp hadn't been on, she would have been able to see her way without the flashlight. But she'd brought it for protection, not illumination. Even after Michael's murder, she couldn't bring herself to buy a gun, but she had always made sure a weapon was near at hand. Back in L.A., she kept a baseball bat under her bed, but she hadn't brought it with her because she wanted to believe coming back to Arcadia would alleviate her fears.

But she would never escape them, Shelby realized now. All she could do was learn not to run from them.

Downstairs, she slipped from room to room, checking corners. Making certain doors and windows were locked. Every now and then, she'd stop and listen for the noise, but all was quiet once again.

Her heartbeat was like the distant echo of a native drum, an uneasy rhythm that stirred her darker emotions. Shelby was afraid, and she didn't want to be afraid.

In the kitchen, she stood for a moment, gazing out the window. Moonlight glistened on water. The river was calm, the night peaceful, but Shelby's heart would not be still. The longer she stood at the window, the harder and faster it thudded.

She wanted to turn and go back upstairs to the safety of her bed, but somehow she couldn't make herself do it. She couldn't tear her gaze from the river.

And then the sound came again, this time beneath her feet.

Thump…

Something was moving about in the dark space underneath the house, bumping against the wooden trunks and storage boxes….

Scrape…

As if dragging something into its lair…

Shelby's mouth went completely dry. The noise was steady now, and louder, but still she couldn't move.

Thump, scrape. Thump, scrape.

The night outside seemed so ordinary. Moonlight on water. The hoot of a distant owl. But there was something very wrong in the darkness.

The clock in the living room chimed. Midnight. The hour when monsters stirred.

Thump, scrape.

And then complete silence.

It was gone.

Shelby didn't know how she knew the danger had passed, but somehow she did. Somehow she sensed that whatever had been under the house had moved on. She searched the darkness outside the kitchen window. Nothing stirred. Not even a shadow.

Still her heart pounded inside her. Her feet would not move from the window.

She stood that way for endless minutes, her eyes glued to the darkness, waiting, watching. Nothing moved. Nothing came back.

A dog, she tried to tell herself. A raccoon, a squirrel, even rats. Any number of animals could have caused the noise.

Call Nathan, a little voice whispered inside her.

No. She couldn't trust him. She was on her own. She had to figure this thing out for herself.

Chapter Nine

As always, daylight did wonders to restore Shelby's calm. Standing at the kitchen window again, this time with sunlight warming her face and a cup of coffee cradled in her hands, she could almost convince herself the noise she'd heard last night had been nothing more than an animal scurrying about underneath the house, building a nest or foraging for food perhaps.

The notion that the intruder had been human, someone deliberately trying to frighten her, seemed less likely in the light of day. While it wasn't so hard to imagine that her uncle James would enjoy scaring her all the way back to California, his tactics were usually more direct—like walking into the office and pronouncing his plans to have her grandmother declared incompetent. That was a threat Shelby took very seriously, and she supposed it wasn't inconceivable that James might try to bolster his claim against her grandmother by proving how unstable Shelby was.

Still, she had a hard time picturing her elegant uncle, in his designer clothing, skulking about in the dirt and cobwebs beneath the house. It would have been a simple matter, after all, for Shelby to have gone outside and shone a flashlight in the space, catching him in the act. Unless, of course, he was banking on her inability to do so.

Maybe he suspected she would be too frightened to do anything but cower inside. He already knew about her nightmares, the time she'd spent in the hospital after Lunt's attack. Her stint in the psychiatric ward had only been a couple of days, but James had made it sound as though she'd gone off the deep end.

And who was to say she wouldn't have if Dr. Minger hadn't intervened? His soothing, nonjudgmental demeanor had made it possible for Shelby to confide in him her terror, not just of Lunt, but of losing her grip on reality.

If I'm not going crazy, why do I keep dreaming about a monster?

Because we all need our monsters, Shelby. They help to explain the darkness in our world. Sometimes it's easier to believe in such creatures than to admit that bad things happen for no good reason.

Maybe that was what she'd done twenty years ago, Shelby mused, staring out the window at the river. Maybe it had been easier back then to be frightened of a creature that came up out of the river rather than to face her deepest terror—that her own parents didn't love her.

Time and adulthood had helped to vanquish that particular monster, and Albert Lunt was still in prison. There was nothing to be afraid of now. There was no good reason why Shelby shouldn't go outside and check underneath the house for signs of an intruder—animal or human.

Certainly nothing *inhuman* would be lurking any-where other than in the realm of her imagination, she told herself firmly, as she went out the back door and down the back steps.

The only access to the space beneath the house was a gate in the latticework underpinning. It wasn't fastened securely, and for a moment, Shelby consid-ered the possibility that the gate banging back and forth could have caused the noise she'd heard. But then she remembered there hadn't been a wind last night. Not even a gentle breeze.

Tentatively, she drew back the gate and peered inside. The space was just as she remembered it— packed tightly with boxes, trunks, lawn mowers, a garden tiller and several other pieces of machinery. Her grandmother never liked to throw anything away.

Shelby had brought along her flashlight, and now she switched it on, letting the beam pick out the deepest corners and the shadowy crevices between the boxes. She could detect nothing amiss, and judg-ing by Miss Scarlett's lack of concern for Shelby's proximity to the darkened space, she thought un-likely she'd find a litter of kittens stowed nearby. The cat lay on the back porch, dozing in a patch of sun-light.

Switching off the light, Shelby started to turn away, but then she noticed something glistening on the inside of the door. She bent to take a closer look, then instinctively recoiled when she realized what she was seeing. A tingle of unease ran up her back-bone, and she shivered in spite of the warm sunshine.

Opalescent in the sunlight, a series of large fish

scales had been embedded in clumps of dried mud left behind on the door.

"HAVE YOU GIVEN any more thought to the story we discussed the other day?"

Virgil had summoned Nathan into his office at the worst possible time. The newsroom, always bustling with people coming and going—some with legitimate business, but most without—was even more chaotic than usual.

And to top it all off, Nathan hadn't gotten much sleep last night. Every time he closed his eyes, he would see Shelby's anguished face, the look of betrayal in her eyes, and he would realize all over again what a mistake it had been to ask her for an interview.

"Well?" Virgil prompted. "Have you talked to Shelby or not?"

"She won't agree to an interview," Nathan said flatly.

Virgil lifted a brow. "So? She'll come around if you keep after her long enough. I seem to recall you could talk her into just about anything when the two of you were kids. Weren't you the one who got her to go down to the river that night in the first place?"

Come on, Shelby. If we see the monster, my uncle Virgil will put our picture in the paper.

They were to have met on the bank at midnight, but Nathan hadn't shown up because he'd instinctively known, even at the age of ten, that he needed to be home. His mother had left the night before, and his father was in a bad way.

And besides, he'd never really thought Shelby

would actually go down to the river alone. That she'd see something she thought was the Pearl River Monster rising out of the water.

He thought about what Gayla Weathers had told them yesterday. *He always believed you,* she'd said to Shelby. *He never thought you'd made that story up, like some of the others around here did.*

And then, *He never claimed he saw it. It was more like a feeling he got when he was diving, he said. Like something was watching him. A presence, he called it.*

Nathan rubbed the back of his neck, trying to rid himself of a sudden disquiet. What if Danny Weathers and Shelby were both right? What if there *was* something in that river?

It would be a hell of a story, that's what.

Don't be an idiot, he chided himself. Experts had combed every inch of the river after the monster sightings that summer, especially when Shelby's claim had been so compelling. They'd found nothing.

And yet, Nathan had an inkling of what Danny Weathers had been talking about. Far below the surface of the river, he'd felt that odd sense of displacement himself, that spine-tingling panic that something not quite of this world lurked on the muddy bottom.

Wouldn't hurt to look up some of those experts now, Nathan decided, jotting a note on the legal pad he always kept at the ready. Maybe in addition to their expert opinions on monsters and mutant species, he could pick their brains about what Takamura might be up to.

He glanced at his uncle. "I don't think it's a good

idea to press her on this. She might pull the Pearl Cove's ads, and we can't afford to lose the business."

Virgil scowled.

"Besides, I need to talk to you about something else. I could really use your help," Nathan said, deliberately changing the subject.

"Well, sure." Virgil looked pleased by the request. He motioned to the chair across from his desk. "Have a seat."

"Thanks, but it won't take that long." Nathan paused, figuring out the best way to proceed. "I saw some of my mother's old columns in the morgue the other day. I was wondering how long she worked at the paper."

"Only about a year." Virgil's gaze was suddenly shadowed with sorrow. "Her leaving like that is what killed your daddy, you know."

Technically, Nathan's father had dropped dead of a heart attack five years ago, but Nathan suspected his uncle's summation wasn't all that inaccurate. Caleb Dallas never did get over his wife's betrayal.

"Why didn't he ever try to find her?" Nathan could still picture his father sitting alone night after night at the kitchen table, his head bowed, hands trembling. His only solace a bottle of whiskey. "Why didn't you help him?"

"I would have, if he'd asked me." Virgil ran his fingers through his thick, cottony hair. "Katherine left of her own accord, Nathan. It wasn't my call to go tracking her down. Besides. I thought it might be for the best."

Nathan frowned. "How do you figure that?"

Virgil sighed. "Your mama came from a well-to-do family in Memphis. She was an only child, pampered, spoiled. She came to Arcadia one summer to visit a relative and that's how she and Caleb met. Back then, your daddy was…" Virgil waited for the right words to come to him. "Dashing, I guess would be the best way to describe him. He always worked outside, so he was bronzed and muscled. A great big hulk of a guy. I think he just kind of bowled your mama over, as she did him. Katherine was a very beautiful girl. They eloped a week after they'd met."

A memory came back to Nathan suddenly. He'd been sitting on the front porch with his mother late one afternoon, waiting for his father to get home from work. His mother was barefoot, and she wore a sleeveless summer dress, badly faded and out of style, but somehow elegant on her. Nathan could still remember the glitter of the tiny diamonds that surrounded the pearl pendant she always wore at her throat and the shimmer of sunlight in her dark hair as she told him how she and his father had first met, how it had been love at first sight. But looking back, Nathan realized that even while she'd been talking about love, there'd been a terrible melancholy in her eyes, a tremor in her voice.

Why do you look so sad, Mama?

Because I have to tell your father something. Something that will make him very sad.

She must have been contemplating leaving that very day, Nathan realized.

For a long time after she'd gone, he hadn't wanted to trust anyone. He hadn't wanted to believe in love, and it was for precisely that reason he'd never told

Shelby how he felt about her. He'd been too afraid of losing her. So he'd said nothing in all the years they'd known each other, and when she'd grown up, she'd gone off to California to marry someone else.

"Those two just weren't meant to be." Virgil shook his head sadly. "Katherine was accustomed to having nice things, clothes, a big house. Caleb couldn't give her any of that." When Nathan started to protest, his uncle hastened to add, "Now, don't take that the wrong way, son. I loved your daddy. Caleb was a good man in a lot of ways, but he never did have much ambition. He was content to eke out a living on the river, but it just wasn't enough for your mama. I don't mean any disrespect by saying this, but I'm glad you didn't turn out like him, Nathan."

No, he hadn't turned out to be like his father. If anything, Nathan had had too much ambition, and look where it had gotten him. He suddenly felt almost fiercely protective of his dead father's honor. "Dad was the hardest-working man I've ever known. He would have done anything for his family. Are you saying my mother left him to go off with someone who had money?" Even after all these years, what she'd done still hurt Nathan more than he wanted to admit. He was a grown man. He'd made his own share of mistakes. But somehow he'd never been able to bring himself to forgive his mother for her betrayal, so for years he'd simply chosen to put her out of his mind.

"I don't know who she ran off with," Virgil admitted. "You read the note yourself, Nathan. She didn't mention his name. I don't expect it was any-one from around here.''

"Do you think she went back to Memphis?'' That city was only a two-hour drive from Arcadia. How ironic it would be if his mother had been that close all these years.

Virgil gave him a piercing look. "Why all these questions about your mama, all of a sudden? You never used to talk about her at all.''

Nathan shrugged. "I was just a kid when she left. I didn't want to think about what she'd done. Now I guess I'm starting to wonder why she did it.''

"I told you that already.''

"You told me what you think. Maybe I'd like to hear it from her.''

"What are you saying, Nathan?''

"That I might like to try and find her.''

Virgil's gaze seemed full of pity. "After all these years? What would be the purpose, son?''

"Maybe to lay some old ghosts to rest. I don't know.'' Nathan scrubbed at his face with his hands. "Maybe if I'd had a chance to say goodbye...'' He trailed off, not wanting to finish his thought.

But it was there in the back of his mind. If he'd had a chance to say goodbye to his mother, maybe his life would have turned out differently. Maybe he wouldn't have felt so driven.

Don't lay your mistakes at her doorstep, a little voice warned him. *That fiasco in Washington was of your own making.*

"Maybe you're right,'' he said wearily. "Maybe it wouldn't serve a purpose.''

"What's done is done," Virgil said sagely. "Some things are best left to the past."

"Yes," Nathan agreed. "I'm sure Shelby feels that way, too."

SURREPTITIOUSLY, Shelby studied Delfina as she waited on an elderly customer. The girl was surprisingly adept as a saleswoman. With Shelby, she was shy and retiring, hardly voicing more than a sentence or two all day unless Shelby struck up a conversation with her. But as Delfina helped the customer choose from a display of pearl rings, her lyrical voice carried through the quiet store. The woman was having a hard time making a decision, and Delfina appeared to be patience personified.

As she watched her, Shelby tried to imagine the young woman going into the office, opening the vault, and taking her grandmother's pearls. When Delfina spoke of Annabel, it was with the utmost reverence and affection. Shelby couldn't believe Delfina could be so duplicitous, but the fact remained that several pearls were missing, and until the culprit was apprehended, Shelby had to suspect anyone associated with the store.

The thought had hardly formed in her head, when the bell over the front door tinkled softly and her uncle James walked in, accompanied by a tall, broad-shouldered man in a dark green silk suit. The stranger carried an expensive-looking briefcase in his right hand, and on the pinkie finger of his left glowed a huge cabochon-cut ruby. His dark hair was combed back from his face and fastened at his nape in a ponytail that curled over his collar. Shelby suspected immediately that he was James's attorney, but his flashy attire—not to mention his enormous physique—seemed more suitable for someone associated with a crime syndicate than a law firm.

James, as always, was dressed immaculately in a beautifully cut navy suit. The only jewelry he wore was a gold Rolex on his wrist. He nodded curtly to Shelby as they crossed the shop to the counter where she stood.

"Hello, Uncle James."

He ignored the greeting and shot a frowning glance in the direction of Delfina and her customer. "We need to talk in private."

He didn't wait for Shelby to acquiesce, but instead stepped behind the counter and led the way back to Annabel's office. Shelby had little choice but to follow. The man with the briefcase at least had the courtesy to allow her to precede him.

He closed the door behind them, and Shelby had the uncomfortable feeling that she'd just let herself walk into an ambush. She was alone in her grandmother's office with two men who could easily overpower her.

For a moment, her breath quickened and she put a hand to her throat, feeling the rush of her pulse beneath her scarf. Then, quickly asserting control over her panic, she walked briskly around the desk, putting the walnut expanse between her and her visitors. "What can I do for you?"

"This is my attorney, Walter Kincaid. We've come to talk to you about Mother."

"What about her?"

"Shall we sit?" the lawyer suggested in a deep,

liquid voice. He smiled at Shelby, but the almost blinding whiteness of his teeth did nothing to reassure her of his character. She was willing to bet money he was as unethical as his client, but it was always possible appearances could be deceiving.

She nodded toward the two chairs across from the desk and then took a seat herself. Adjusting the scarf at her throat, she said calmly, "I know why you're here, Uncle James, and I'm warning you, I won't stand for it. If your intention is to have Grandmother declared mentally incompetent, I will fight you tooth and nail. I've done some research. It's not as easy as you seem to think to be awarded guardianship of someone's finances, especially when that someone is as sane as you or I."

"On half of that we can agree."

Shelby wouldn't allow herself to react to his taunt. "What do you want from me?"

"I'd like for us to come to an agreement." He paused, gazing at her with eyes as blue as her own. "I don't want to hurt Mother, but I can't allow her to be taken advantage of. As her son, it's my duty to look out for her best interests. You're not qualified to run this store, Shelby, much less be entrusted with the huge inventory of pearls Mother has acquired. If you won't step aside of your own accord, I'll have to take steps to have you removed."

"Removed?" she said angrily. "Grandmother asked me to come here and run the shop while she's recuperating. How can you just disregard her wishes like that?"

"That's my whole point. I'm afraid she isn't capable of making a decision like that." The concerned look on his face might have been laughable if the situation didn't have the potential for such devastating consequences.

Shelby glared at him. "You won't find anyone in this town willing to testify against her."

"I'm afraid you're mistaken about that," the lawyer interjected smoothly. "We have several witnesses to her—shall we say?—lapses."

"What *lapses*?" Shelby asked coldly.

"Mother has become quite forgetful." James smoothed his silk tie, a casual motion that blatantly denied the mock worry in his expression. "Just last month, she misplaced several valuable pieces of inventory. She even went so far as to file a police report, then the jewelry turned up in one of her desk drawers where she'd put the pieces and forgotten about them."

Alarm darted through Shelby, but she tried to keep her expression neutral. Was it possible her grandmother had misplaced the loose pearls as well? Was that why she'd been so adamant that Shelby not go to the police?

Shelby didn't like the train of her own thoughts. There was nothing wrong with her grandmother's mind. Everyone was allowed lapses of memory once in a while. After Michael had been killed, Shelby had often had trouble remembering what day of the week it was. But that only enhanced James's point. Both Annabel and Shelby had problems.

"I won't allow you to do this to Grandmother." She pinned her uncle with icy contempt. "Even if you have no chance of winning, think what such a legal proceeding would do to her."

James's eyes flickered, but Shelby doubted it was with guilt. He glanced at his watch. "Consider this fair warning, Shelby. If you pack up and go back to California, all this will be forgotten. If you stay, you'll force me to drag both you and Mother into some very unpleasant business."

"I'm not going anywhere." Shelby rose, bracing herself against James's anger. "So I don't think we have anything further to discuss."

James and his attorney stood as well. Walter Kincaid smiled at her once again as he strode out of the office, but her uncle paused at the door. "You shouldn't have come back here, Shelby."

"I came because Grandmother asked me to."

"No. You came because you were running scared, just like always. But you better watch out, little girl. One of these days, that monster's going to catch you."

He turned then and laughed as he walked out the door.

THE LAST PERSON Shelby expected to see at the shop that afternoon was Nathan, but when she glanced up from her work and saw him standing in the office doorway, she momentarily forgot about her uncle's threat, the missing pearls and even her midnight intruder.

Suddenly all she could think about was the way Nathan's lips had felt so warm and promising against hers last night. The way he'd smiled down at her...the fact that he'd wanted to kiss her again.

"Delfina said I could come back. May I come in?" His eyes were dark and smoldering as always, but his expression was a bit wary, as if he was none too sure of his welcome.

His apparent uneasiness made Shelby remember something else. The reason for the kiss. The reason he'd wormed his way back into her life. Because he wanted a story.

She gazed at him for a moment, marveling at the way her heart raced at his nearness in spite of what she knew about his motives. In spite of the fact that he had betrayed their friendship and she wanted nothing more to do with him.

Clearing her throat, she said, "I suppose you can come in for a minute. I'm very busy, though."

"I understand." He walked into the office, but instead of taking a seat, he came over to her desk and stood gazing down at her. "It's a madhouse over at the paper, too, but I had to take a minute to come by and see you. I want to apologize."

Up close, his eyes were even more intense than Shelby remembered. No flecks of gold. No hints of green. Just a warm, dark, velvety brown as he stared down at her. She could see the faint shadow of his beard, and it gave him a reckless, dangerous air. He'd always had a heedless quality about him, an adventurous spirit, even as a boy. But as a man, those attributes were almost lethal.

And Shelby was just a little too lonely. A little too vulnerable.

She frowned, trying once again to shore up her defenses. "No need to apologize. Just promise me you'll never print a word about me in your paper."

"You know I can't do that."

"*What*?" Anger warred with her attraction. "Are

you telling me you're still going through with that story after I told you how I felt? You're simply going to disregard my feelings?''

"I never said that. Look." He paused. "I'm doing everything I can to put that story on the back burner for now. I don't want to proceed until and unless you give me your permission. But I can't promise to never print a word about you. I'm in the news business, Shelby, and I can't pick and choose the news as I would articles of clothing. That's not how it's done. I have a responsibility to the paper and to its readers.''

"My life is no one else's business," she said bitterly.

"I can understand why you feel that way, but you're wrong. When you told Sheriff McCaid you'd seen the Pearl River Monster, your story became a matter of public record. Your claim had the potential to affect a lot of lives, not just because of a real or imagined threat, but because people have a right to know what's happening in their own backyard. My uncle had a responsibility to this community to print your story. And I'm sorry to say that when Albert Lunt killed your husband and then attacked you, the public had a right to know that as well.''

"That doesn't sound like much of an apology to me." She folded her arms stubbornly. "It sounds like an excuse to ride roughshod over people's lives.''

"I'm sorry you feel that way.''

"I do." She drew a long breath. "So I really don't see that you and I have anything else to talk about.''

"I disagree." She started to protest, but he didn't give her time. "Just hear me out. If I'm not going to go with the story about you, then I have to concentrate on Takamura. And for that, I need your help.''

"My help?" she asked incredulously. "Why would I want to help you?"

"Because in spite of everything, I'd like to think we're still friends. We've been through a lot together, Shelby.'' He came around the desk and leaned against the side. Shelby wished he would go back around to the other side. She didn't want him standing so close to her. She didn't like being able to reach out and touch him, if she wanted to. She didn't like feeling so tempted.

"Shelby," he said softly. "Look at me."

She didn't want to do that, either, but his voice was so deep and smooth and so richly compelling, she had no choice. Almost against her will, she lifted her gaze to his, and the moment she did so, her heart began to beat in short, painful strokes

This couldn't be happening. Not to her. It wasn't fair. It was too soon.

He reached down and took her hand, and Shelby let him. His skin was warm against hers, and she imagined she could feel the blood pounding through his veins in a crazy staccato. She knew hers was.

"The reason I asked you to dinner was because I wanted to spend time with you, not because I wanted a story."

"Are you saying you *didn't* want a story?" Her voice was a breathless challenge, and Shelby hated the sound of it. It gave away too much of what she was feeling.

"If you'd said yes, I would have written the story," he admitted. "And it would have been a good one. But I told you once I would never ask you to do something you really didn't want to do. Remember?''

She gave a barely perceptible nod.

''So no story until you give me the okay. That's what I came here to tell you.''

''And to ask for my help,'' she reminded him. ''Although I still don't know what I can do.''

''I'm coming to that.'' Letting go of her hand, he walked over to the window and leaned against the frame. ''We got sidetracked last night. I never finished telling you about my association with Danny Weathers.''

''You said you'd followed him one night, but I assumed it was because he worked for Takamura.''

''He was my contact inside Takamura Industries.''

''Contact?'' The word conjured up images of clandestine meetings in back alleys and seedy hotel rooms. In Arcadia? Shelby had a hard time believing it. ''You mean he was feeding you information about Takamura?''

''That was the idea, but he didn't really know much about the lab. Or so he said. After seeing his wife's reaction, I have to wonder.''

''So why did you follow him?''

Nathan shrugged. ''Reporter's instinct, I guess. I thought he was holding out on me about something. We met at the river a couple of nights before he was killed, a spot not too far from the lab, and he seemed agitated. Excited. He even went so far as to say that if Takamura found out what he was up to, there'd be hell to pay. I assumed he meant talking to me. Anyway, after we both drove off, I had a hunch that I should go back and take a look around. As it turned out, Danny had doubled back, too, and he was in his diving gear. I hid out to see what he was up to.''

"What happened?" Her anger forgotten, Shelby rose and walked over to the window to stand beside Nathan.

He glanced down at her. "Nothing much. He dove for half an hour or so, and then came back up and left. I couldn't figure out what he was up to then, but after our conversation with Gayla, I think we need to check out that spot for ourselves."

"Wait a minute," Shelby said anxiously. "I never agreed to help you with anything other than research. I certainly never said anything about diving."

"You won't have to. Just keep watch while I go down."

"And do what if Takamura shows up?" she demanded.

He gave her a reluctant grin. "Run like hell!"

"You can pretty much count on that."

But in spite of her blithe talk, Shelby had no intention of keeping watch for Nathan while he dove. His proposition sounded a little too familiar. A little too much like the ones he'd involved her in when they were kids. The kind that had always ended with skinned knees, bruised egos or worse.

She had a feeling this scheme would definitely fall into the "or worse" category.

Chapter Ten

Shelby stood on the bank and watched Nathan ready himself for the dive. It was not quite dark, but the shadows cast by the cypress trees and water elms crowding the water's edge gave the landscape an eerie, somber feel.

Or maybe it was just her nerves, she thought. She still couldn't quite believe she'd allowed Nathan to talk her into this. She should have been home by now, having a nice, peaceful dinner with Miss Scarlett.

Nathan had already donned his wet suit and was checking the gauges on his air tank. Strapping it on, he gave Shelby a thumbs-up sign. "All set."

"I still don't know what I'm doing here," she said into the hushed silence. "Supposing someone from Takamura Industries does come by. What can I do? Throw rocks at them?"

"Consider yourself here for moral support." Nathan glanced at the river and frowned. He didn't seem all that anxious to plumb the murky depths, and Shelby couldn't blame him. She could think of very few things she would enjoy doing less.

"Are you sure this is the right spot?" she asked him nervously.

He nodded and pointed toward the opposite bank. "Danny was directly in line with that crooked cypress tree over there when he went down. I have a feeling he used it as a marker."

"Even if it is the right spot, how are you going to see anything? It's almost dark and the water's so muddy."

"I've got this." He pulled out an underwater light from his equipment bag. "It should help some." He took another long look at the river. "Okay. It's now or never."

"Wait," Shelby said in near-panic. "What if you run into trouble down there? How am I supposed to help you?"

"If I'm not back up in thirty minutes, send down a search party."

If he was joking, Shelby wasn't laughing. "I'm serious, Nathan. I don't think this is a good idea."

"Relax. I'm a pro at this, remember?" He reached for his mask. "Wish me luck."

"Luck." Shelby rubbed her hands up and down her arms where chill bumps had suddenly popped out. "And be careful."

He adjusted his mask, then, fitting the regulator into his mouth, walked slowly into the water. They could have taken a boat out to the middle, but Nathan thought that might draw unwelcome attention. He'd chosen instead to enter the water from the bank.

Within seconds, he'd disappeared underneath the surface, leaving a trail of bubbles floating on top of the water. After another moment, the bubbles vanished, too.

Shelby glanced around. The twilight deepened with every second, and with the darkness came the mosquitoes. A cloud of the pesky insects swarmed every inch of her exposed skin, and for a moment, she distracted herself by hastily applying another layer of repellent. That accomplished, she had nothing to do but stare at the river and wonder what was happening below.

Any number of things could go wrong. Nathan could get tangled in a fishing net or line, and she'd never know it. There were snakes in the river. The giant alligator snapping turtles he dreaded so much. Shelby couldn't blame him. The hideous-looking creatures, with their massive heads and ridged shells, resembled some holdover from prehistoric times, and they could be extremely aggressive.

Shelby suppressed a shudder as she glanced at the luminous dial on her watch. How long had he been down? No more than ten minutes. He still had plenty of air, although he hadn't expected to be down for long. Just a quick look to see if further investigation was worth their time.

Their time, Shelby thought. How easily she'd slipped back into her role as Nathan's sidekick. His partner in crime, her grandmother would say. How easily she'd forgotten that only last night, she'd considered their friendship beyond repair.

But he'd promised—no story unless she agreed—and Shelby had no reason to distrust him. Nathan had never lied to her.

And if she were honest with herself, she'd have to

admit that she *wanted* to trust him. It would be nice to believe there was still someone in this world she could count on.

She realized the fear had been creeping over her ever since Nathan had disappeared beneath the surface of the river, but she'd been trying to ignore it. Trying to pretend that her concern for Nathan was causing her heart to beat faster and faster as a cold chill danced along her spine. But now, with an almost dreaded certainty, Shelby realized she was no longer alone. Someone—or something—was watching her from the shadows.

The sensation was so strong, the hair on the back of her neck stood on end.

Her mouth dry with fear, she turned to scan the twilight behind her.

DIVING IN THE Pearl River had always been considered a little like diving into hell. Visibility was poor at best and nil at worst. The slightest movement stirred up the silt and mud until even the most powerful light couldn't penetrate the gloom. Nathan was completely blind, and as he tried to hang motionless in the water, waiting for the muck to settle, he ran through a litany of possible hazards. The treacherous currents could play havoc with his sense of direction. He could be snagged by a fishing line with razor-sharp hooks.

The light was able to cut through the muck now as the visibility cleared. He descended to the bottom and moved slowly through the water, taking care to keep his hands and flippers out of the mud.

Twenty feet below the surface, the Pearl River was

a strange, primeval world. Giant roots tangled with one another to form a surreal maze through which the skeletal limbs of trees occasionally beckoned. Long stems of grass waved ghostlike in the current, and the darting movement of a fish stirred a long trail of silt across the bottom.

The light sparked off a beer can rooted in the mud and made Nathan recall going out on the river with Ray and Bobby Joe Buford the night they'd found Danny Weathers. He thought about Danny diving in this very spot, moving slowly through the water as Nathan was doing now. Looking for mussels. Perhaps experiencing that peculiar sensation of being watched he'd told his wife about. Nathan felt it, too, that odd, spine-tingling sense that something lurked in the water just behind him. Or over him.

He rolled in the water, swinging the light around. Nothing was there. Just his imagination.

He concentrated on his breathing again. Slow, easy. In, out. Don't waste air. Don't get excited.

For God's sake, don't panic.

He moved forward slowly as the light tunneled a narrow canyon in the gloom. Something huge lurked in the water just ahead, and he stopped so abruptly, his flippers grazed the bottom. A whirlwind of silt drifted upward, along with a burst of air bubbles caused by his panic.

For the longest moment, he couldn't see anything. His heartbeat thundered in his ears. His breathing was heavy and rushed, but he couldn't slow it down. Something was down there with him. He could feel that same preternatural presence Danny Weathers had spoken of.

A cold fear climbed Nathan's spine, but he forced himself to remain perfectly still, waiting for the silt to settle once again. He kept his light trained on the same spot, and when the water finally cleared, he swam slowly toward the dark, hulking shadow.

A car.

Pushed in the water years ago, probably to collect an insurance settlement.

Nathan didn't know whether to be amused or angry with himself. It wasn't like him to be so easily unnerved, and yet there had always been something about this river…about the vulnerability of being almost blind in a strange and dangerous environment.

He regulated his breathing, then used the light to check his time and air. He could barely see the gauges, but common sense told him he hadn't been down more than twenty minutes or so. He still had time.

He checked the gauges anyway.

Angling the light on the car, he moved toward it. It was an old model, probably from the fifties. The door on the driver's side hung open, as if whoever had pushed the car into the water had jumped out at the last minute. The vehicle had obviously been parked on the river bottom for decades. Nothing unusual about it except…

That feeling again.

A sensation of being watched.

A strange premonition that there was something in this water that didn't belong.

Nathan swam toward the car, almost expecting to see the skeletal remains of the driver still trapped behind the wheel.

But it was empty.

He played the light along the inside. The interior had an almost tomblike quality about it.

He pushed away, feeling suddenly chilled.

Moving around the car, he focused his attention on the muddy river bottom, looking for the mussel bed Danny Weathers had found. Had his recent windfall of pearls really come from a secret mussel bed, or had he stolen the gems from Takamura?

Or could they somehow be the missing pearls from Miss Annabel's store?

Down here, in a world unto itself, it probably wasn't a good idea to think ill of the dead. Better to concentrate on the task at hand.

Nathan reached the back of the car and paused, searching the river floor. Something brushed against his arm and he jerked. The light arced crazily. Out of the corner of his eye, he saw the beam spark off something near the trunk, but it was only an impression. He was more concerned at the moment with what had touched his arm. A fish, he hoped, not a loggerhead. Not anything supernatural.

Realizing he'd been holding his breath, he drew in a slow, steady drink of oxygen. His heartbeat slowed. The water cleared. He played the light over the trunk of the vehicle, then moved in closer, letting the tomblike atmosphere of the car settle over him. Pulling himself over the rear fender, he angled the light downward. The lock on the trunk must have been broken before the car had been sent to the bottom of the river because the lid had been wired shut. He wondered if the metal cable was what had sparked in the light. He bent closer, trying to get a better look, and the moment he did so, something bumped hard against his shoulder.

He lost his grip on the light and it fell to the bottom, stirring the silt into an impenetrable cloud. Nathan was completely blind and he knew, without a doubt now, he wasn't alone in the water.

The moment the silt cleared, he grabbed the light and swam away from the car.

He didn't know what had bumped into him, didn't want to know.

He'd been down a long time. His air supply was bound to be getting low.

Without checking his gauges, he turned and started the slow journey to the surface.

SHELBY COULDN'T SHAKE the feeling that she was being watched. She didn't want to be anywhere near that riverbank, but she didn't dare leave. Nathan had been down a long time. What if he'd run into trouble? She wasn't sure what she could do to help him, but there was no way she would desert him.

Glancing over her shoulder, she scoured the darkness again. Twilight had come and gone, and night settled over the river in a quiet hush. The lightning bugs were out now, darting among the cypress trees that, like deformed gnomes, squatted by the bank. Shelby tried to divert herself by picking out faces in the knotted wood, but in the moonlight, they seemed a little too lifelike. A little too eerie.

Where on earth was Nathan? If he didn't come up soon, she'd have to decide on a course of action. Go for help. Swim out into the river and see if she could find him herself.

Would she even have the nerve to jump into that muddy water?

She should never have agreed to such a foolhardy scheme. It was dangerous to swim in the river alone, much less to dive. She didn't care how much experience Nathan had. She envisioned him on the bottom, trapped in a fishing line, his air slowly ebbing away—

A movement in the middle of the river caught her eye, and Shelby held her breath, watching as the surface began to bubble. Something dark popped up out of the river, and for a moment, a memory rose inside her.

For so long she'd pushed that night out of her mind, but now it came back to her in a flash. Her terror. Her feeling of utter helplessness as she'd watched the water churn and boil, and then something horrible had topped the surface. The monster—

The memory slipped back into the farthest corners of her mind as she realized a far more deadly danger lurked nearby. The sound of a boat engine echoed across the water, growing steadily louder by the second. Someone had the throttle wide open.

Shelby's heart began to beat a terrified rhythm as she watched Nathan bobbing in the water. He was swimming slowly for the bank, but he was still in water deep enough for a boat. And Shelby didn't think he'd heard the engine, perhaps because his ears were still adjusting to the pressure change. In desperation, she jumped up and down, waving her arms and yelling for him to hurry.

The boat seemed to explode around a bend in the river, the powerful engine louder than a buzz saw. It was moving without lights, cutting a dark silhouette across the water as it headed directly for Nathan.

Shelby screamed a warning. She ran into the water, plunging waist-deep as she waved her arms frantically. She didn't know if it was the brilliant sparkle of moonlight on the boat's wake or the sound of the engine that finally attracted Nathan's attention. He'd inflated his buoyancy compensater and for a moment, he floated in the water, scouring the darkness. Then he spotted the boat.

"Go under!" Shelby screamed.

But he couldn't. The BC kept him afloat. There was nothing he could do but float helplessly in the water. Shelby watched in horror as he struggled with the BC, and then, at the last moment, he rolled in the water, until only his tank remained on the surface. The boat roared by, missing him by inches. Barely easing back on the throttle, the driver cut a breathtaking one-eighty.

Nathan was still working at the BC. He had his knife out, but within seconds, the boat was almost upon him again. Shelby screamed his name as he finally plunged underneath the water.

Was he safe? Had he been able to dive deeply enough? Too close to the surface and the prop would slice right through him. The way it had Danny Weathers.

The boat turned again, fishtailing water. Heading back. When Nathan didn't surface, the driver opened throttle and sped away.

Shelby had no idea whether or not Nathan was injured. As she struggled to get out of the water, her feet slipped from under her. She must have been standing on the very edge of an underwater precipice the whole time, for now she was submerged in deep water. She couldn't touch bottom.

Startled, it took her a split second before she began to fight her way back to the surface.

Only then did she realize she was caught.

Something had fastened itself around one of her ankles—a tree root, a fishing line, *something*—and held her trapped under water. No matter how desperately she struggled, she couldn't break free.

A silent scream rose in her throat as the black, mind-numbing panic she'd come to dread washed over her.

She was going to die!

She was trapped only inches from the surface of the water, only a few feet from the bank, but she was still going to die.

Albert Lunt was going to win after all.

Images tore through Shelby's mind. Of Lunt. Of Michael.

Of Nathan.

In death, she could be with Michael. For a split second, she considered it. Then it was gone.

With the reality of her own mortality facing her, Shelby knew she wanted to live.

Battling frantically to free herself, she plunged more deeply into the water, reaching blindly for whatever it was that held her imprisoned. She had no idea if the boat had come back. If Nathan was safe. She only knew that she had to get free. She had to have air.

Her lungs screaming, Shelby fought the panic engulfing her as ferociously as she fought the water.

But the harder she struggled, the more futile the effort.

As the precious seconds ticked by, her strength ebbed.

She couldn't fight anymore. She couldn't.

Through the haze of lethargy, she heard someone calling her name. A familiar voice that ordered her to fight. Demanded she live. Michael? Nathan?

Shelby could see a dark gaze staring deeply into hers. Could feel the warm comfort of loving arms as she was lifted and carried to safety.

For a moment, she thought it was all a dream, and then her head broke the surface, and she automatically began to pull air deeply into her lungs. Coughing and sputtering, she felt the muddy river bottom beneath her feet and then she and Nathan were both stumbling out of the water and collapsing on the bank.

"Are you all right?" He'd flung off his mask and tank and was bending over her in the near-darkness. "Shelby?"

"I'm fine," she managed, still gasping for breath. "My foot was caught—"

"I know," he said grimly. "It's a miracle I found you. When I came back up and saw you'd disappeared from the bank, I didn't know what to think. I knew you wouldn't leave. Not of your own accord." In the rising moonlight, his face looked ghostly pale, but his eyes were darker than ever.

So close to death, Shelby's thoughts had been consumed by images of Nathan. Somehow in that one, precious moment, everything had changed for her. Now she understood exactly what her grandmother had been trying to tell her. *A year or five years. Or thirty years for that matter. What difference does it make? Michael is gone, but you have the rest of your life.*

Shelby drew a long, trembling breath, wanting to reach out to him, wanting to tell him about the profound revelation that might have changed the course of her entire life, but the time wasn't right. He'd almost been killed, too, and Shelby had no way of knowing what life-altering apocalypse he might have undergone. One, perhaps, that didn't include her.

"Did you see who was driving the boat?" she asked him instead.

"No. It was too dark, and it all happened too fast. Did you see anything?"

She shook her head. "Only that he was deliberately trying to hit you. I think he was trying to kill you, Nathan."

"I think you're right," he agreed darkly. He got to his feet and reached a hand to help her up. "Let's get the hell out of here before he decides to come back."

BACK UP on the road, where Nathan had left his Bronco, he quickly changed from the wet suit into dry clothes, and then a few moments later, they were pulling up in Shelby's driveway. He walked her to the house, and Shelby didn't offer a protest. Not for anything in the world did she want to enter that darkened house alone.

Thank goodness, Nathan seemed in no hurry to leave. Once they were inside she turned in the foyer to face him. "I'm going upstairs to get out of these wet clothes, but I won't be long. Can you stay?"

He looked a little surprised by the invitation, but he nodded without hesitation. "Sure. I think it might be a good idea if we talk over what just happened."

Fifteen minutes later, Shelby emerged from the bathroom dressed in clean jeans and a T-shirt. Her short hair was still wet from the shower, but instead of taking the time to blow it dry, she tucked it carelessly behind her ears. Nathan had just seen her covered in mud and slime from the river. Damp hair wasn't likely to bother him.

She found him in the kitchen, sitting at the table. He glanced up when she walked in, his gaze moving over her in a way that just a day ago would have made Shelby uncomfortable. It still made her nervous, but in a different way. She wanted to return his perusal, and she did, letting her gaze search his face, roam the breadth of his shoulders and the taut muscles in his arms.

Nathan seemed taken aback by her new boldness. "Uh, I found root beer in the refrigerator," he said, indicating the frosty cans he'd placed on the table. "You think your grandmother might have something stronger?"

"I'm quite certain she does." Shelby walked over to a cabinet and opened the door to scan the shelves. "She always says that a true Southern woman is never without a good bottle of bourbon on hand."

"Miss Annabel always was a woman after my own heart." Nathan moved up behind Shelby and reached over her to procure the bottle of whiskey that was just out of her grasp. As he did so, his body brushed up against hers, and an awareness, as hot and keen as lightning, streaked through Shelby. Every nerve ending in her body seemed to stand on end, and she had to resist the urge to lean into him, to prolong the contact. To make it even stronger.

He handed her the bottle. "You do the honors."

Her hands trembled slightly as she got down two glasses and added a dollop of whiskey to each. Nathan took the bottle from her and added a good deal more. "Cheers," he said, lifting the glass.

The whiskey made Shelby's eyes water, but the fire in her stomach was instantly fortifying. She took another sip, then another.

Nathan grinned. "Amazing what a little whiskey can do at a time like this."

Shelby nodded and sat down heavily at the table. "A little more, and I might not remember that someone tried to kill you tonight."

"And you."

She looked at him, startled. "I was trapped in a fishing line or a tree root. Or something. It had nothing to do with the boat."

"You didn't see anything?" Nathan probed.

There was an odd glimmer in his eyes that Shelby didn't think was caused by the whiskey. "What do you mean?"

He shrugged. "I don't know. I had this weird feeling while I was down there. Like I wasn't alone."

Shelby's spine tingled with fear. "You mean like another diver was down there with you?"

Their eyes met, and for the longest moment, Nathan didn't say anything. He lifted his glass and took another long swallow of whiskey. "Yeah. I guess that's what I mean."

But it wasn't. For the first time since she'd known him, Shelby knew that Nathan was deliberately lying to her. Something had happened underneath the surface of the river, but for some reason, he was reluctant to talk to her about it.

"What happened down there?" she asked softly.

He frowned. "Nothing. Really. It was just a feeling."

"That you weren't alone."

He shrugged again. "The river's always been a creepy place. Especially on the bottom. There's a strange, *Twilight Zone* feel to it so that even ordinary things take on a supernatural quality. There was an old car down there." He paused, taking another sip of his whiskey. When he set down the glass, he was frowning again. "I could have sworn the damned thing was haunted."

"The car?"

When he didn't answer, Shelby stared at him for a moment. She'd never seen Nathan like this. When they were kids, he'd always worn his bravado like a badge of courage, picking fights with bullies he knew could whip him with one hand tied behind their backs. Swimming farther out into the river than anyone else simply because he'd been dared. It had been a point of pride with him not to show fear, regardless.

But now...

If something had scared Nathan...

As if sensing her growing unease, he gave a little laugh. "Listen to me. I sound like a superstitious idiot."

"You're entitled," Shelby allowed. "You were almost killed tonight."

"We were almost killed. I'm sorry now I got you into this." His gaze on her grew even darker, so intense that Shelby had to glance away.

"What do you think is really going on around here, Nathan? Danny Weathers was killed after he claimed he'd found a new, productive mussel bed. Now some of my grandmother's pearls have gone missing right after my uncle shows up making threats. And all that strange stuff with Takamura Industries. This place is not like I remembered it."

"Isn't it?" Nathan reached across the table suddenly and took her hand. The tingles up and down her backbone deepened. "There's darkness everywhere, Shelby. You can't run from it."

"I didn't think I was. But in spite of everything that happened to me that summer, I always thought of Arcadia as a safe harbor, a protected refuge in a dangerous world." She gave a shaky laugh. "I wouldn't exactly call it a haven now."

"Are you thinking of going back to L.A.?"

The question was casually spoken, but there was a tautness in Nathan's features that made her think he might be more interested in her answer that he wanted to let on. She turned the question around on him. "Are you going back to Washington?"

"Why would you ask that?"

"Because I don't see you living out your days in a small, backwoods town in Arkansas. You once had big dreams, Nathan. What happened to them?"

"Some of them came true. Some of them fell through. Some of them—" He gave her an odd smile. "I guess the verdict is still out on some of them."

Excitement stirred deep inside her. Was it possible he was talking about her? About them?

Shelby hardly dared believe it could be true. She wasn't even sure she wanted it to be true, because, now that the danger was fading, she remembered all too vividly all the reasons she couldn't get involved with Nathan.

As if experiencing his own sudden trepidation, he finished his drink and stood. "It's getting late. I'd better go and let you get some rest. Besides, I need to get home and get the river washed off me."

Shelby got up and walked him out. Standing on the front porch, they both fell silent for an awkward moment, as if uncertain how to bring such a climactic evening to its proper closure.

The moon was up now, a huge, silvery coin glowing softly over the trees. In the distance, the river was like a shimmering ribbon of gray satin.

Nathan said anxiously, "Are you going to be all right out here? I hate leaving you alone after what happened."

Shelby suppressed a shiver. She couldn't say she was ecstatic about facing the hours of darkness ahead of her, but somehow she'd gotten through sixteen months of such nights. And morning always came. There was a measure of comfort in that knowledge.

"I'll be fine," she said with more confidence than she felt. "Whoever was in that boat wasn't after me. You're the one who should be careful, Nathan."

"I will." He took out a pen from his pocket and jotted a number on a scrap of paper. "I'm living in my dad's old house. If you need to call me, for any reason, here's the number. I can be over here in less than five minutes. And here's my cell phone number as well. Call anytime. I mean that, Shelby.''

''I know.''

Still he hesitated, as if not quite certain what was expected of him. Should he kiss her good-night? Would she let him?

Shelby could almost hear the debate being waged inside his head. She stood holding her breath, not knowing herself what the outcome would be.

Then suddenly he came to a decision, and with a regretful smile, turned and hurried down the porch steps.

Shelby watched him walk across the yard, get in his vehicle, and back out of the driveway. He waved once as he put the Bronco into gear and headed down the road toward home. And still Shelby watched, reluctant to go back inside that empty house and face the prospect of another restless night.

She glanced at her watch. Ten o'clock. Two more hours until midnight.

Turning with a sigh, she reached for the door, but a sound in the darkness stopped her short. Fear shot, icy cold, through her veins.

Chapter Eleven

It was a cat. In trouble, by the sounds of the plaintive cries.

Shelby turned, scouring the darkness. "Miss Scarlett? Where are you, kitty?"

The cry came again, nearby and so mournful, Shelby could no more have ignored the mewling than she could have neglected a child's sobbing. Like her grandmother, she had a weakness for children and animals, particularly those in distress.

Forgetting her own brush with danger earlier, she moved to the top of the porch steps, calling out once more to Miss Scarlett. When the cries came again, Shelby followed the sound down the steps and into the yard. The moon was bright, but the canopy of leaves overhead blocked much of the light. Trying to avoid the deeper shadows, Shelby headed toward the river.

"Miss Scarlett? Here, kitty, kitty. Where are you?"

The cry came again, closer still, and Shelby glanced up. Eyes glowed in the high branches of a pecan tree.

"Miss Scarlett? Is that you?"

The cat's answering meow was less plaintive this time, as if she sensed that rescue was imminent.

"Can't you get down?"

Obviously, she couldn't. The cat stared down at Shelby expectantly.

"Okay. Let me see if I can come up and get you."

Reaching for the lowest branch, Shelby swung herself up, just as Nathan had once taught her to do when they were kids. Grabbing the next limb, she pulled herself to her feet and began to climb.

It was easy going. The branches were thick and close together, but the tricky part was getting Miss Scarlett to turn loose of her perch. At first, she kept backing way from Shelby, but then, having nowhere else to go, the cat simply dug her claws into the tree bark as deeply as she could, refusing to budge an inch. She wanted to come down, but she didn't quite trust Shelby to get her to the ground safely.

"You're going to have to work with me here," Shelby coaxed.

Miss Scarlett merely blinked at her and meowed.

Balancing herself on a sturdy branch and clinging to another, Shelby paused for a moment to reassess the situation. From her lofty roost, she had a breathtaking view of the river. By night, the water was like liquid silver, beautiful and luminescent. Moonlight shimmered pale on the surface, as soft and regal as the glow of fine pearls.

But the fragile beauty was deceptive. The river could also be deadly.

A shiver coursed through Shelby as she thought again of the close call she and Nathan had experi-

enced earlier, and then she marveled at her own re-
silience. She'd faced danger tonight, but instead of
cowering inside her house, here she was, alone and
up a tree, trying to rescue her grandmother's cat. Was
that progress? she wondered. Or a sign that she really
had gone off the deep end?

And did she really want to know the answer to
that question?

She started to turn back to the task at hand, but a
ripple on the river's surface made her pause. Tiny
rings of water undulated in the moonlight, disappearing almost as quickly as they appeared. And then
another occurred and another, as if tiny fish were
jumping in the water.

Shelby watched, puzzled by the phenomena, until
she realized the tiny wavelets weren't being caused
by fish, but by something being tossed into the water.
With a start, she saw someone sitting on the bank.
The figure remained as still as a stone statue, except
for the almost imperceptible motion of her wrist as
she tossed something into the water.

The cascading black hair, gleaming in the moonlight, was unmistakable. Whether or not she'd heard
Shelby calling for the cat earlier, Delfina Boudreaux
seemed unaware of or unconcerned by her presence
now.

Plop. Plop. Plop.

The tiny ripples appeared in the water again.

Shelby frowned. What on earth was Delfina doing?
Shelby had excellent distance vision, and the moonlight was brilliant. Even from this far away, she could
see something glowing, smooth and round, in Del-

fina's hand. She held it in her palm for a moment before throwing it into the water.

A pearl, Shelby thought in shock. If she didn't know better, she'd swear Delfina was sitting on the bank, casting large pearls into the water. She couldn't help wondering if that could be the answer to the riddle of her grandmother's missing pearls. Was Delfina stealing the gems, and then, for some strange reason known only to her, returning them to the river?

With another jolt, it struck Shelby that Delfina was sitting in the exact spot where Shelby had sat the night she'd seen the Pearl River Monster rising out of the water. And just like Shelby, Delfina appeared to be waiting....

Shelby's heart hammered against her rib cage. She remained frozen in the trees, not daring to move, hardly even breathing as she watched Delfina for several long minutes. It didn't matter that Shelby knew what she was thinking was crazy. It didn't matter that she knew monsters didn't exist. She was suddenly consumed with the certainty that Delfina was trying to lure something to the surface.

After what seemed an eternity, the young woman stood and began walking along the water's edge, disappearing into a thick copse of trees. She didn't come back out.

Unable to make sense of what she'd just witnessed, Shelby turned back to the cat. "Come on, Miss Scarlett," she said hastily, reaching so quickly the cat didn't have time to bury her claws. Nestling her securely in the crook of her arm, Shelby began to climb down. Miss Scarlett was surprisingly patient until they started across the yard to the porch, and then she leaped from Shelby's arms and tore off into the shadows, as if whatever had frightened her up that tree might still be lurking nearby.

Uneasy herself, Shelby hurried to the house. Now that the cat was rescued and apparently as feisty as ever, the night's events came back full-force on Shelby, and she glanced nervously around the darkened yard.

The light she'd left on earlier was like a beacon. She hurried toward the porch steps, then paused, staring down. Someone had been here, just moments ago.

Not someone. Some*thing*.

It had left footprints. Not like any Shelby had ever seen before.

Large. Misshapen. Sinister.

The footprints stopped at the top of the steps, as if the porch light had frightened the creature away.

Creature...

Shelby's head jerked around as she frantically searched the darkness. Her heart pounded in terror. Dimly she became aware of the telephone ringing inside the house, but her legs wouldn't move. She couldn't force herself to climb the porch steps. To put herself anywhere near the spoor that *thing* had left behind.

This was crazy.

There's no such thing as monsters, she told herself desperately. A dog had left those prints. A huge, wet dog that had frightened Miss Scarlett up that tree.

Of course.

That had to be it.

But that perfectly logical explanation didn't keep Shelby from hugging the edge of the steps, avoiding the tracks, as she practically leaped to the porch. It didn't keep her from jamming home the bolt on the front door almost violently once she was safely inside.

NATHAN WHEELED into Shelby's drive, shut off the motor and jumped out of the truck. He'd been regretting leaving her alone from the moment she'd disappeared from sight in his rearview mirror. All the way home, he'd worried about her, and his disquiet hadn't abated all through the routine of his evening. He'd gone inside the small, clapboard house he'd grown up in, showered, then grabbed a bite to eat before heading back to the paper. But as he'd neared Arcadia, the fear that Shelby was in danger had grown, had become almost overwhelming each time he'd called her house and got no answer.

Nathan told himself his alarm was unfounded. Shelby was fine. Earlier, on the river, the boat had tried to run *him* down, not her.

Even so, the evening hadn't been without mishap for Shelby. She'd lost her footing in the water and might have drowned if he hadn't found her in time.

The thought of that was worse than a knife blade twisting inside him. If Shelby had drowned with him so close…

Without another second's thought, Nathan had swung the Bronco off the road, made a U-turn, and headed back to her house, traveling at a speed that could easily have led to his own demise.

But something was driving him hard, a certainty

that something was wrong. A fear that he might not be able to reach her in time.

That same fear propelled him across the yard now. By the time the truck door slammed behind him, he was already on the porch. A light was on, and he stood in its glare, pounding frantically on the door.

The lace curtain was pushed aside, and he saw Shelby peer around it, her blue eyes wide and almost dazed-looking. He waited impatiently while she released the dead bolt and drew back the door.

"Nathan?"

"You didn't answer your phone," he said accusingly. "I thought something was wrong."

"You called me?"

"Several times." He strode passed her into the hallway. Quickly she turned and relocked the door.

Something *was* wrong. He could tell by her actions. Her movements were jerky, and she was having a hard time meeting his gaze.

He took her by the shoulders and forced her to look at him. "What's wrong?"

"N-nothing."

"Something is. I can tell. What happened? Are you all right?"

"I'm fine. Really." But her gaze darted away from his.

Her face was much too pale. She had the look of a woman who had been badly frightened, but didn't want to admit it.

His grasp on her tightened. He could feel her trembling beneath his hands. "Talk to me, Shelby."

"It's nothing," she said, backing away from his

hold. But her gaze went back to the front door, as if to reassure herself it was bolted.

"I don't believe that. Something frightened you."

"Well, of course, something frightened me!" she said almost desperately. She turned away, wringing her hands. Nathan doubted she was even aware how much of her emotional state that nervous gesture gave away. "Someone tried to run you down with a boat. I almost drowned. Is it any wonder I'm a little...uneasy?"

She was more than a little uneasy. Any fool could see that. What Nathan couldn't figure out was why she wouldn't level with him. "I should never have dragged you into this mess," he said harshly.

She gave a helpless shrug. "You didn't know what was going to happen. How could you?"

"I never believed Danny Weathers's death was an accident. I should have been more careful."

"It's over and done with now," Shelby said wearily. "I'll be fine by morning."

But Nathan wasn't convinced that that would be the case. She was still holding out on him, and he hated to think it might be because she didn't trust him. "What happened, Shelby?" he asked softly. "Why can't you tell me?"

To his amazement, tears blurred her eyes suddenly. She turned away, but he caught her arm. "Is it James?"

She looked almost startled. "James? No. At least...I don't think so."

Nathan's concern suddenly morphed into anger. He stared at Shelby, frowning deeply. "If he's bothering you, threatening you in any way, you tell me right now. I'll take care of James.''

She smiled a little at that. ''You said that same thing twenty-one years ago, remember? You threatened to punch him in the nose after he told your uncle that I'd lied about…what I'd seen in the river.'' The smile disappeared, and she glanced away again.

''I meant every word of it.''

''I know that. You've always wanted to protect me, but you can't. I have to find a way to protect myself.''

Her words bothered Nathan in a way he couldn't explain. They seemed so ominous. ''You've always been able to take care of yourself. If I ever doubted it, I sure as hell don't now. Not after what you've been through.''

She glanced back at him, her eyes haunted. ''I didn't lie about what I saw that night,'' she almost whispered.

''I never thought you did.''

''But you had to wonder.''

Her eyes glimmered now with an emotion Nathan recognized only too well, and he wanted more than anything to reach out to her, to help her through whatever it was that tortured her tonight. He knew, perhaps better than anyone, what a terrible thing self-doubt was. ''What are you getting at, Shelby?''

She hesitated, putting a trembling hand to her face for a moment. ''You said you never thought I lied, but you couldn't have thought I saw…a monster. Not really.''

"I never doubted for a minute that you saw something you thought was the Pearl River Monster."

"But that's different. Don't you see? You believed I saw something, but you never believed in the monster. I did."

"A lot of people did. Still do. The river's a—"

"Spooky place. Yes, I know. Everybody thinks so." She glanced up at him. "But not everybody sees...things."

So that was it. She'd seen something in the river tonight that had scared the bejesus out of her.

Nathan swore under his breath. "That's my fault, too. All that talk about something being down there with me while I was diving. Another presence. I should have kept my mouth shut."

She glanced at him reproachfully. "I'm a grown woman, Nathan. You shouldn't have to censor what you say to me, like a child who's terrified of the dark. Of creatures that aren't real."

"What brought all this on?" he asked gently.

She turned away, walking from the hallway into the living room. For a moment, she seemed headed for the windows, but then reversed her steps and walked over to the fireplace instead. She stood in front of the empty grate, as if trying to warm herself by an invisible flame.

Nathan followed her inside. For several long moments, she didn't say anything. Then she gazed at him hesitantly. "Did you see anything...out of the ordinary when you came up the porch steps?"

"Like what?"

"Footprints."

"Footprints?"

She nodded and drew a deep breath. "After you left earlier, I went out to find Grandmother's cat. She was stuck in a tree. It took me a while to get her down, and when I came back to the house, I saw wet tracks on the porch steps."

"Maybe we'd left them earlier," Nathan suggested. "You were soaking wet when we got home."

Shelby shuddered. "Trust me, I didn't leave these tracks."

Nathan didn't like the sound of that. If Shelby had had an intruder, it might be connected to the incident with the boat. Maybe the driver had spotted her on the bank and recognized her.

"Why didn't you tell me about this when I first got here?" he demanded.

"Because I didn't know…" She trailed off, as if she didn't want to finish her thought. "I'd just seen Delfina down by the water, but I don't think she could have made the tracks, either."

"Delfina? What was she doing here?"

"I'm not sure," Shelby said, looking even more uneasy. "I don't think she saw me."

"You stay put," Nathan said. "I'm going outside to have a look around."

"Nathan—"

Shelby crossed the room and took his arm. It was the first physical contact she'd initiated with him since she'd come back, and Nathan couldn't help wishing that it was out of something other than fear. But, hell. He'd take what he could get.

"I'm going with you," she said.

He started to argue, but he could see the determination in her eyes, and he realized this was something she needed to do. Shelby was always one for facing her fears.

"Okay," he said. "Let's go."

Chapter Twelve

"They're gone." Shelby stared down at the porch steps. They were completely clean and dry.

Nathan bent down and touched the surface. "The concrete feels a little damp, but I don't see any tracks."

"They were there. I swear it."

"I believe you."

"Do you believe me, or do you believe that *I believe* they were there?" she asked doubtfully.

He glanced up at her in surprise. "Why would you ask that?"

"It's obvious, isn't it?" She folded her arms. "It's possible I imagined the footprints. Just as I imagined seeing a monster a long time ago. You wouldn't believe the things I imagined after Lunt attacked me. Sometimes in the hospital, I was so sure he'd found a way to get out of jail, I knew if I opened my eyes, I'd find him standing over my bed. I imagined it so strongly that I was admitted to the psychiatric ward." Shelby hadn't meant to blurt out that little intimate tidbit, but once the words were spoken, she couldn't take them back. Couldn't deny the truth.

How would Nathan feel about her now? she thought with an inward wince.

He stood slowly and came up the steps, just far enough so that their gazes were on the same level. "I know all about that," he said softly.

Shelby drew back in shock. "You *know? How?*"

His gaze never flickered from hers. "I overheard you and James talking in your grandmother's office the other day. It made me realize how much of a bastard he still is."

"You aren't...disgusted?" She was almost afraid to look at him now, afraid to see the pity that he was bound to feel.

"Why would I be disgusted? Or even shocked for that matter? Shelby." He took her chin gently and turned her face to his. "Your husband had just been brutally murdered. The psycho who shot him stalked you for weeks. He killed your dog, and then he broke into your house and attacked you with a knife. Yes," he said, when she gave a startled protest. "I know all about that, too. I guess what I find shocking is how you managed to survive. How you came through it as well as you have."

"I wasn't crazy," she said almost defensively. "I was having nightmares. Bad ones. And I had some sleepwalking episodes. I'd never done that before, but the doctors agreed the sleeping disorders were triggered by severe trauma. I was moved to the psychiatric wing for a couple of days at my doctor's request and kept sedated, so that I could get some rest."

"Sounds reasonable to me."

"Does it?" Her tone sounded challenging, even to herself.

"Sure it does." Nathan took her arms. "Come on. Let's go back inside."

Shelby glanced back down at the steps. She *had* seen footprints. Huge ones. But they were gone now.

She shivered as she and Nathan went back inside the house. Without a word, they walked into the living room, and Shelby sat down heavily on the sofa, almost too weary to think straight. But that was the whole problem, wasn't it? She hadn't been thinking straight when she'd seen those wet tracks on the porch steps, or when she'd conjured an image of the creature that might have left them.

No rational person would imagine such a thing. No sane person would even think it.

Nathan moved across the room to the aquarium and stood watching the fish. She said to his back, "There's something else you need to know about me."

He turned to face her. "You don't have to tell me anything you don't want to."

"It's not a secret. Until I moved back here, I'd been seeing a psychiatrist for months."

He shrugged. "Nothing unusual about that. I've considered seeing one myself once or twice."

She glanced at him, astonished. "*You?* I can't believe that. You've always been the most self-possessed person I've ever known."

He gave a self-deprecating laugh. "Maybe as a ten-year-old kid." He sobered. "I've done some things in my life that might shock *you,* Shelby. Might even disgust you."

She found that hard to believe, too. "You mean what happened in Washington?"

He lifted one eyebrow. "You know about that?"

"Only that you made some mistakes."

"That's putting it mildly." He turned back to the aquarium.

"Do you want to talk about it?" she asked softly.

"Maybe someday." He glanced at her over his shoulder. "We're talking about you right now."

She ran her fingers through her short hair. "I'm sick of talking about me."

He turned at that and moved across the room to sit beside her. "Twenty-one years ago, you saw something come up out of that river. Something that terrified you. I've never doubted that for a moment."

"But I couldn't have seen what I thought I did. It's not possible. Just like those footprints tonight..." She trailed off, glancing away. "You know, if James gets wind of this, he'll use it against Grandmother. You can't say anything to anyone, Nathan."

"I wouldn't do that."

He wouldn't. She knew that.

Shelby glanced back at him, and for a moment, their gazes locked. In the aftermath of fear, her senses were keenly heightened. It seemed to her that Nathan's hair had never gleamed more darkly. His eyes had never seemed so deeply mysterious. She let her gaze linger on his before moving it over the angles and planes of his face, the strong line of his jaw, his lips.

They were parted slightly, waiting to kiss her. She remembered the feathery brush of his mouth against hers, a touch so light, she'd been left wanting more. Wanting what they'd shared in her dream.

Anticipation surged through her. If he kissed her now, which would it be? A mere whisper or a breathless plunder?

He moved toward her.

Shelby's breath caught.

And then the clock on the mantel chimed midnight. She jumped, badly startled, and the spell was broken.

Her laugh was shaky. "I didn't realize it was so late. We both have to work tomorrow. I'm fine, Nathan. Really." His lips still seemed just a little too kissable, and so she stood.

He gave her a long, slow appraisal, as if he knew exactly what she was doing. "I know you're fine. But I thought I might stay here tonight anyway."

"What?"

"On the couch." He rose and stood before her. "How long has it been since you've had a decent night's sleep?"

She sighed. "I don't know. I can't remember the last time."

"Then let me stay. You stood watch for me earlier, now let me do the same for you." When she started to protest, he said, "It's the least I can do. I got you into this mess."

"No, you didn't. You didn't put those tracks on the porch steps."

His gaze on her deepened. "But if I'd been here, it might not have happened. And if I hadn't stood you up twenty-one years ago, you wouldn't have had to go through what you did. I owe you."

"I've been on my own for a long time, Nathan."

"I know that." He brushed his knuckles down the side of her face, a gesture that stirred Shelby's emotions. Her memories. She'd been alone and so very lonely. But with Nathan…

With Nathan she felt safe. And she had not felt safe in a long, long time.

"For my own peace of mind, let me stay. Just for tonight." His fingers whispered against her hair. "Let me watch over you. Anything comes up out of that river, it'll have to get through me first."

NATHAN COULDN'T GET to sleep. He'd lain awake for so long that the subtle nuances of the house—the weight settling on the stilts, the tick of the mantel clock, the soft hum of the water filter in the aquarium—barely registered with him anymore. Even the sluggish rotation of the ceiling fan couldn't lull him to sleep.

Lying on his back, he stared at the slow movement of the blades as he thought back over the events of the evening.

If Shelby had had a prowler earlier, the logical suspect in Nathan's mind was her uncle. James wouldn't bat an eye at a little terrorism if it helped him get his hands on Miss Annabel's money.

But there was no reason for him to have been driving that boat earlier. No reason for him to be after Nathan…unless he thought Nathan stood in his way of getting to Shelby. That was a possibility, albeit a distant one.

All right, Nathan silently reasoned. What if James was somehow connected with Danny Weathers? Another slim possibility, but it was a bit coincidental that Danny had come into a booty of pearls at the same time some of Miss Annabel's had gone missing.

Supposing James had stolen the pearls from his own mother, stashed them in an airtight container underwater for safekeeping, and Danny had stumbled upon the cache. That provided a motive. The killer—James—was protecting his plunder.

The car on the bottom of the river, easily accessible with diving gear, would be the perfect hiding place. And there had definitely been something strange about it. Something not quite right.

Nathan frowned, remembering the tomblike atmosphere surrounding the submerged vehicle.

Everything was connected somehow. He knew it. Just as he knew that the answers he sought were there, somewhere, hidden on the bottom of the river.

NATHAN HAD JUST gotten to sleep when a noise roused him. Pushing back the quilt Shelby had laid out earlier, he sat up and glanced around his darkened surroundings. Beyond the arched entranceway of the living room he could see the foyer. A shadow stirred on the stairs.

His heart quickened as he rose. He'd taken off his shirt and shoes earlier, and he moved across the wood floor on bare feet, pausing at the doorway to peer out.

Dressed in white satin pajamas, Shelby descended the stairs and moved as silently as a ghost across the foyer. Turning the bolt, she drew back the door and stepped onto the porch.

"Shelby?"

She didn't turn when he called her name. By all indications, she was completely unaware of his presence.

He followed her out to the porch. She paused at the rail, gazing at the river.

"Needed some air, did you?" he asked her softly.

She still didn't answer him. Didn't even glance his way.

It hit Nathan then that she didn't answer him because she didn't hear him. Or see him. She was still asleep.

He took her arm gently. "Shelby?"

She glanced up at him then, her blue eyes blank and dazed. A chill went through Nathan. It was eerie the way she looked up at him, not seeing him. For a split second, she even reached out her hand toward him.

Then she turned and started down the porch steps.

Again Nathan followed her. There was dew on the grass. He felt the coolness against his bare feet as he trailed Shelby across the yard. He thought at first she was headed for the river, but she turned suddenly and started back toward the house.

As he watched her climb the porch steps, his gaze dropped to the wet footprints she left behind on each stair.

NATHAN COULDN'T get the glazed look on Shelby's face out of his mind that morning. The newsroom was even more hectic than usual because a summer flu had taken its toll on his meager editorial staff. But as busy as he was, Shelby's sleepwalking remained front and center in his mind. There had been something so strange, almost eerie, about the way she'd moved through the darkened house, unaware of his presence or her surroundings. If he hadn't been there, Nathan hated to think what might have happened. What if she'd gone down to the river and fallen in?

It wasn't safe for her to be alone while she was so obviously under stress. But he wasn't at all certain he could convince her to let him stay with her another night. In spite of everything that had happened to her, Shelby valued her independence.

And then, of course, there was the matter of the footprints she'd seen last night. Had the tracks been real or only imagined? Nathan felt guilty for even doubting her story, but after witnessing her sleepwalking, he had to wonder if it was possible that she'd fallen asleep, gone outside without knowing it, and then, when she awakened, saw footprints she herself had left behind.

But she'd insisted the tracks were huge, which gave Nathan considerable pause. It wasn't inconceivable that a large animal had climbed those steps and been frightened away by the porch light. He hadn't mentioned this to Shelby, but just last week, a local woman had seen a bear in her front yard. Could that same bear have paid Shelby a late visit?

"Hey, Nathan! You've got a call on line two," someone shouted.

The receptionist was also out sick, and all those left in the newsroom were taking turns grabbing the phone.

Nathan picked up the receiver and cradled it

against his shoulder while he scanned copy on his computer screen. "Nathan Dallas."

"Mr. Dallas, this is Yoshi Takamura."

Nathan almost dropped the phone. He juggled it for a moment before he got a firm grip on it. "Mr. Takamura. What can I do for you?"

"You've been wanting to see me, I understand." The man's English was flawless. Nathan had heard somewhere that Takamura had come to the United States thirty years ago. In that time, he'd obviously become very Americanized. In spite of his rather formal manner, he even had a faint drawl.

"Your secretary is a hard nut to crack," Nathan said. "You've trained her well."

"Myra takes her duties very seriously," Takamura agreed. "If you're still interested in an interview, I can see you at one-thirty today."

"Uh, that'd be fine. One-thirty it is."

"I'll have someone meet you in the lobby and show you around the offices before you come up."

"What about the lab?" Nathan pressed.

There was a long pause. "Perhaps, on one condition."

"Name it."

"You bring along Mrs. Westmoreland's granddaughter."

"You mean Shelby?"

"Yes. I would very much like to speak with her."

About what? Nathan wanted to ask, but he figured he'd better not press his luck. Instead he said, "I can't make any promises, but I'll see what I can do."

"Thank you, Mr. Dallas."

'No. Thank *you*.'' But the line had already gone dead in Nathan's ear.

SHELBY GLANCED UP from her work, startled to see Nathan in the doorway.

"Delfina said I could come back," he explained. "Got a minute?"

"Of course." When he was seated across from her desk, she said, "You were gone when I woke up this morning, so I didn't get a chance to thank you for staying last night. I can't tell you how wonderful it felt sleeping through the night like that. I don't think I so much as rolled over until morning."

He gave her an enigmatic glance. "Uh, actually, you did."

Shelby stared at him in surprise. "I did? How do you know?"

"You were sleepwalking last night."

An icy chill slipped up her spine. She was sleepwalking again? That wasn't a good sign. "Are you sure?"

"Pretty sure." Nathan gave her a worried look. "You don't remember coming downstairs and unlocking the front door? You don't remember going outside?"

She gasped. "Outside? I went outside?"

He nodded, his expression grim. "You got all the way out to the yard, and then, for some reason, you turned and came back inside."

"What did I do then?" she asked almost fearfully.

"Nothing. You just stood at the bottom of the stairs for a moment, so I picked you up and carried you back to bed. I don't suppose you remember that, either.''

Nathan had carried her to bed? It seemed so strange that she couldn't even remember what, under normal circumstances, could have been a very intimate act. But she could imagine it. All too well. Nathan lifting her in his strong arms, carrying her against his hard body, putting her to bed. She shivered again, hardly daring to meet his gaze.

''Thank you,'' she murmured.

He shrugged. ''No need to thank me. But I do think we should discuss what happened. It's not a good idea for you to be alone at night right now. You're obviously under stress. What if you'd gone farther than the yard and I hadn't been there?''

He didn't say it, but Shelby knew what he was thinking. What if she'd gone down to the river? Fallen in? Drowned without anyone ever knowing what happened to her?

It wasn't an impossible scenario. She'd had a close call in the water just last evening. The river's danger was not something she could afford to take lightly.

But what was he suggesting?

His gaze on her deepened. ''I think it would be a good idea if I spend the next couple of nights or so with you, make sure you don't have any more sleep-walking incidents. It'd make me feel better knowing I was there to keep an eye out.''

Having Nathan as her nighttime guardian would make Shelby feel better, too. But that was the problem. She was finding it a little too easy to rely on him, and if she'd learned anything since her husband's death, it was that she'd better not count on anyone but herself. What if something happened to Nathan?

Shelby wasn't certain she could go through that kind of pain again. She'd finally pulled herself together, but it hadn't been easy. And to deliberately risk her heart again, to deliberately open herself up to the same kind of hurt—

She just wasn't sure she could do it.

Wouldn't it be better to take her chances alone?

"Nathan—"

"Look, I know what you're thinking," he said softly. His eyes were very dark and very deep this morning, and with little effort, Shelby knew she could lose herself in them. "But I'm not asking anything of you. I don't expect anything. All I want to do is make sure you stay safe."

"I know. It's just— "

"Promise me you'll at least think about it," he said. "If not for your own peace of mind, then for mine."

"All right." She toyed with the ends of the turquoise scarf she'd tied at her throat. "I'll think about it."

"Fair enough. Now for my next proposition." He rose and walked over to the desk, leaning against the side. "Feel like a little diversion today?"

She glanced at him doubtfully. "What kind of diversion?"

"A visit to Takamura Industries. We've got an invitation."

She lifted a brow. "How did you manage that?"

"Takamura called me out of the blue this morning

and agreed to give me a tour of the lab—on one condition.''

''Which is?''

''That you come with me.''

Shelby's mouth dropped in astonishment. *''Me?* I've never even met the man. Why would he want me to come?''

Nathan shrugged. ''Your guess is as good as mine, but I'd bet it has something to do with the Tubb collection. What do you say? You game?''

A question straight from their past. Even after all these years, the answer sprang automatically to Shelby's lips. ''Do you dare me?''

Nathan grinned in surprise. ''Yeah, I just might at that.'' He walked around the desk and placed his hands on the surface, leaning toward her. ''In fact, I double-dog dare you. I *triple*-dog dare you.''

''Oh,'' Shelby said. ''That's serious.''

''Well?''

She gave him a smile. ''Why not? I'm feeling a little daring today.''

''Oh, really? In that case—'' He bent toward her so quickly, Shelby didn't have time to pull away. He kissed her hard and fast on the lips, and then he broke away, gazing down at her with another kind of challenge.

Shelby was dazed by the contact. The kiss had been over with so quickly, she hadn't had time to respond. But she'd wanted to. Oh, how she'd wanted to! The feel of Nathan's lips pressing against hers, the hint—just the merest whisper—of his tongue inside her mouth had sent a jolt of awareness through her body and had let her know, in no uncertain terms, that her libido was very much alive and kicking.

"Shelby?" Nathan's gaze turned curious. "What's the matter? Still not what you were expecting?"

She cleared her throat. "Uh, no. Not exactly."

It wasn't a lie. She hadn't expected to like it so much.

THE BUILDING that housed Takamura Industries was unimpressive on the outside, just an unattractive two-story brick affair with small windows, a gravel parking lot and a covered walkway that led down to a boat dock and the laboratory—and even uglier building that squatted at the river's edge.

A young Japanese woman met Shelby and Nathan in the lobby. Introducing herself as Yoshi Takamura's niece, she took them on a tour of the building, recounting in flawless English Takamura's long history in the pearling industry. His family had been pearl farmers in Japan for many years. When the business became so competitive, Takamura moved to America, wisely predicting that the exploding pearl markets in Japan would drive up the price of freshwater mussel shells.

With her long, glossy black hair and exotic features, Miki Takamura reminded Shelby of Delfina. She wondered if Miki was just as mysterious.

She led them out a back exit of the building and along the walkway to the lab. The inside of the structure was not at all what Shelby had expected—no pearls growing in test tubes or petri dishes that she could discern. No strange creatures suspended in slimy liquids. Instead, the room contained rows of long metal troughs filled with water so murky it had to have come straight from the Pearl River.

Miki reached down in one of the tubs and withdrew a large mollusk. Nathan walked over and examined it in her hand.

"Your uncle is culturing freshwater pearls?"

"Not exactly. None of the mussels in these tanks has produced or will ever produce a pearl."

"Then what is the nature of your work here?" Shelby asked curiously.

Instead of answering, Miki returned the mollusk to the water, then dried her hand on a paper towel. "Did you know that a hundred years ago, mussels were so plentiful in the Pearl River you could walk knee-deep into the water and fill huge sacks from one spot? They were called muckets, and the pearls that grew inside were collected and sold, sometimes in quantities that would easily fill a teacup."

Miki paused. "My uncle's dream is to restore the river to that same productivity. The mussel beds, as you know, have become badly exhausted due to pollution, dredging, the damming of the river. In another few years, the species may become extinct unless a way can be found to genetically strengthen its resistance to pollution and to the colder waters caused by the dams. In that, we have succeeded." She waved her hand toward the tanks. "But the genetically-altered mussels don't produce pearls, even when an artificial irritant is inserted. So our work continues."

She shrugged as she said this and motioned for them to follow her out of the lab. "I'll take you up to see my uncle now."

"Wait," Nathan said. "I've got some questions I'd like to ask you. Is your uncle funding the research himself or is the government subsidizing the experiments?"

Miki glanced at him noncommittally. "I'm sure my uncle will be able to answer all your questions." Meaning, she had no intention of doing so.

They backtracked along the covered walkway into the building, and she led them up the stairs. At the end of a narrow hallway, she knocked, then opened the door and spoke briefly to the occupant. After a moment, she stepped aside for Shelby and Nathan to enter, then closed the door behind them.

Yoshi Takamura rose and came around his desk to greet them. He wasn't what Shelby had expected, either, although she couldn't say she'd actually formulated a mental image of the man her grandmother so despised. But if she had, she would have pictured him as large and overbearing, a man who got what he wanted through intimidation.

Mr. Takamura was none of these. He was short and thin, with silver hair and an unassuming and dignified demeanor. He bowed slightly over each handshake, his dark eyes surprisingly warm.

"Please sit," he said, indicating the chairs across from his desk. In all the times she'd lived in Arcadia, Shelby could remember having had only one brief glimpse of Mr. Takamura—on the day he'd driven away from her grandmother's house, leaving Annabel stewing over his offer. It wasn't that he was a hermit or a recluse, but over the years he had kept to himself, which had no doubt contributed to the mystique and rumors that surrounded him.

"You have questions, Mr. Dallas," he said, but his gaze was on Shelby.

"I'm interested in the work you're doing in the lab," Nathan said. "Why have you kept the experiments such a secret?"

"So far we have produced nothing but failure." Mr. Takamura didn't elaborate, but Shelby thought she understood him. He was a private man. He would want neither his failures nor his triumphs to be the source of speculation. In spite of everything she'd heard about him from her grandmother, Shelby felt a strange sense of kinship with him, a feeling she couldn't begin to explain.

"Would you be willing to answer questions about Danny Weathers's death?" Nathan asked him.

He trained his gaze on Nathan. "Danny's death was a tragic accident."

"I'm not so sure it was. An accident, I mean."

Mr. Takamura's expression sharpened, but he said nothing.

"Have you talked to Danny's widow?" Nathan pressed.

"Yes, to make the arrangements. As the spouse of one of my employees, she is entitled to a death benefit. I wasn't certain she was aware of Danny's policy, and I didn't want her to be worried about financial matters at a time like this."

Was that the reason Gayla had been so reluctant to talk to them about Takamura? Shelby wondered. Not because she suspected him of anything sinister, but because she was worried about losing his goodwill?

"I assure you, Mr. Dallas, I know nothing more

of Danny's death than what I've been told by Sheriff McCaid. But if you would like to continue this conversation at some later date, I would be happy to accommodate you. For now, however, I've kept my end of the bargain. I've provided you a tour of the facilities, including the laboratory. In return, I would ask for the opportunity to speak with Mrs. August in private.''

Nathan glanced at her, lifting one eyebrow. "Shelby?''

She nodded. "It's okay.''

But Nathan didn't appear to relish leaving her alone with Mr. Takamura. He rose hesitantly. "I'll wait outside for you.''

After he'd left the room, Mr. Takamura leaned forward in his chair, folding his hands on his desk. His gaze on Shelby was dark and piercing, but not at all threatening.

"I wanted to speak to you about your grandmother,'' he finally said.

"What about her?''

"It is my sincere hope that after our conversation, you will be willing to intercede with her on my behalf.''

Shelby gazed at him, puzzled. "You mean about the Tubb collection?''

He waved an impatient hand. "I have no desire to acquire the Tubb collection or any collection. Aside from my work in the lab, I'll be retiring at the end of the year.''

"Then I'm confused,'' Shelby said. "If you don't want Grandmother's pearls, why have you been trying to buy them for so many years?''

He gazed at her wearily. It seemed to Shelby that his expression suddenly became indescribably sad. "Because it was the only way I knew how to approach her. Annabel and I both speak the language of pearls."

Shelby stared at him helplessly. "I'm afraid I still don't understand. What is it you want, Mr. Takamura?"

"Your grandmother's hand in marriage."

Shelby remained speechless for at least thirty seconds. To say that he'd taken her by surprise would have been a gross understatement. "W-what?" she finally managed to sputter.

"Perhaps I should tell you a little about my background." He settled back in his chair. "I moved here thirty years ago to start my business. I was forty-five years old, alone. Not a young man. My wife had died years before, and we had had no children. I'd resolved myself to dedicating my life to my occupation. And then, unexpectedly, I met your grandmother. Our paths crossed because of our mutual love of and fascination for pearls. We had so much in common, it seemed only natural that we would gravitate to one another. Become friends." His gaze flickered. "She was a widow, but her loss was more recent than mine. She hadn't had time to recover, to accept her husband's death. He'd only been gone a year or so then, and she was still in deep mourning. I think she began to somehow feel threatened by our friendship."

"Threatened how?"

He hesitated. "That I might somehow take her husband's place in her heart. You see, it was friendship for her, but for me, it was love at first sight. I'd never met anyone like Annabel. But when I realized it was too soon for her, I retreated. I waited. A year passed, and then another. Then five, and still she refused to acknowledge what I believed—what I have always believed—was between us. In time, she even managed to convince herself that I was her enemy, that I had almost single-handedly destroyed her beloved river. You see," he said softly, "that's why I've devoted myself to saving it. To restoring the Pearl River to what it once was. For Annabel."

Shelby couldn't believe what she was hearing. All these years, Yoshi Takamura had loved her grandmother? Still loved her?

Sometimes fate just has plain bad timing, Shelby. A year or five years. Or thirty years, for that matter. What difference does it make?

Her grandmother's words came back to Shelby now. Had Annabel been thinking of Yoshi Takamura that day? Had her advice stemmed from her own experiences, her own regrets?

Shelby stood. "I hardly know what to say, Mr. Takamura."

"It's a shock," he acknowledged. "I understand that. But time is running out for us. We're not young, your grandmother and I. Her accident brought that home to me. Who's to say how many years we have left to us?"

Who was to say how many years any of them had left? Life could be snatched in the blink of an eye from even the very young.

Shelby knew that only too well.

Chapter Thirteen

"Well? How'd it go?" Nathan asked anxiously once she met him in the parking lot.

Shelby hardly knew where to start. She was still in shock from Mr. Takamura's revelation, but she also found herself smiling. "You're not going to believe what he told me."

Nathan immediately perked up. Shelby could almost see the reporter's gears grinding inside his head. If he thought she was going to deliver him a hot story, he was going to be disappointed, she thought. He certainly wouldn't be expecting a love story.

"Did he pressure you about the Tubb collection?" Nathan asked.

"No. As a matter of fact, he says he's not interested in the Tubb collection or any collection. He's retiring from the industry."

"What?" Nathan scowled down at her. "Then why has he been so persistent all these years about your grandmother's pearls?"

"Because he says feigning interest in the Tubb collection was the only way he knew how to approach her, seeing as how they both speak the language of pearls.''

''What? He didn't really say that.''

''He did, too. I swear.'' Shelby's smile broadened at Nathan's incredulous expression. ''He says what he really wants is to marry Grandmother. And don't say *what*,'' she warned him.

Nathan didn't say anything for a moment. Then, ''Well, I'll just be damned.''

''I know. But if you could have seen his face when he talked about her, Nathan…'' Shelby trailed off, deeply moved all of a sudden. The full implication of Mr. Takamura's confession was only now hitting her. ''Just think about it. For thirty years, he's been carrying around a torch for Grandmother, even though she gave him no reason to believe his love would ever be reciprocated. Can you believe someone could be that devoted?''

Nathan gazed down at her with a strange look on his face. ''Love works in mysterious ways, I guess.''

Something in his voice made Shelby's pulse quicken. ''He said Grandmother came to think of him as her enemy in order to protect herself.''

'She saw him as a threat,'' Nathan murmured.

''What?''

He shrugged. ''Nothing. I was just thinking about something your grandmother told me once.'' He paused, his expression suddenly shuttered. ''So are you going to tell her what he said?''

Shelby nodded. ''I think I have to. It's too important not to.''

''Think it'll make a difference?''

''I don't know,'' Shelby said wistfully. ''Grandmother's been alone for a long time. And she's stubborn. Once she makes up her mind about something, or someone, it's hard to persuade her to the contrary.''

''I hear that,'' Nathan said. Then Shelby could have sworn she heard him mutter, ''What is with you Westmoreland widows anyway?''

THEY STOPPED at Willie's Boathouse for a quick bite to eat before going back to work. Over catfish po'boys and fries, Nathan told Shelby what he'd found out about her uncle.

''I just got a call from a source while you were in with Takamura,'' he said. ''And it might interest you to know that your dear ol' Uncle James has been making frequent trips to Tunica, Mississippi.''

''Tunica, Mississippi?'' Shelby echoed. ''What's there?''

''You're been away from here for too long, Shelby,'' he chided her. ''You've missed the gambling explosion in some of our bordering states.''

''Are you saying James has a gambling problem?''

Nathan speared a french fry with his fork. ''I don't know if it's a problem, but it's certainly a possibility as to why he's so desperate for money. Here's another little tidbit my source managed to dig up. James has applied at the bank for a loan, and get this. He's using his own private collection of freshwater pearls as collateral.''

''His own private collection?'' Shelby said in shock. ''What collection? He's never been the least bit interested in pearls, only the profit they generated.''

"That's what I thought."

Nathan watched as anger turned Shelby's cheeks bright pink. "Those are the missing pearls, Nathan. I'd bet you anything. James has a key to the shop because he let himself in the other morning. For all I know, he has the security alarm code and the vault combination as well."

"That seems pretty likely," Nathan agreed. "On the other hand, it could be that he somehow got his hands on your grandmother's private collection. She kept those at home, didn't she? Have you seen them since you've been back?"

Shelby frowned. "No, but I haven't looked, either. I don't even know where she keeps them these days, but I know she never used to take any special precautions." She paused, her eyes still glittering with anger. "You're right. It would have been easy enough for James to get into the house after Grandmother had gone to the hospital and taken the whole collection."

"That still wouldn't explain the pearls missing from the vault," Nathan pointed out.

"I'm inclined to believe that he took those, too, but I guess it could have been Delfina."

Nathan glanced at her in surprise. "Why would you think Delfina took them?"

Again Shelby hesitated, as if she didn't want to say anything more. Then she shrugged. "She's had access to the vault, too."

"Why do I have a feeling there's something you aren't telling me?" he asked suspiciously.

She sighed. "Because if I told you what I thought

I saw last night, you'd think it as crazy as the disappearing footprints on the porch steps.''

"I never said I thought that was crazy."

"Not in so many words." She glanced up at him.
There was something in her eyes that disturbed Nathan. "I'm the first to admit my behavior hasn't always been rational these past months."

"And I've told you, I understand why. You're entitled, Shelby. Lighten up on yourself."

"I wish it were that easy," she murmured.

It was obvious she wasn't going to say anything
more on the subject of Delfina, so Nathan decided to
let it drop for the moment. After they finished their
lunch, he paid the bill and they walked back out to
his truck.

As he opened the door for her, he caught her arm
for a moment, and she glanced up at him inquiringly.

"Shelby—" Her eyes were like blue velvet, he
thought suddenly. Soft and sensuous. He moved his
hand up to her face, caressing her jawline with his
thumb, and to his surprise, she let him. She didn't
move away. In fact, he could have sworn she moved
almost infinitesimally toward him.

"Yes?"

He wanted to kiss her. Properly. Taking his time
with her. Slowly and thoroughly until her lips opened
like a flower beneath his.

But there were people around. And Shelby had
always been a very private person. He didn't think
she'd relish being the subject of gossip, and he certainly didn't want to be the cause of it.

So, instead of kissing her, he said almost gruffly,
"You be careful, you hear me? Don't go after James

or Delfina, or anyone else, on your own. You find out anything about those missing pearls, you come to me. Don't try to handle it yourself. You don't have anything to prove.''

She scowled up at him. ''You don't need to worry about that. I may be crazy, Nathan, but I'm not stupid.''

HE DROPPED her back at the shop, and for the rest of the afternoon, Shelby couldn't get her conversation with Yoshi Takamura out of her head. She and Nathan had discussed it at length after they'd left the restaurant, and, after mulling it over, Nathan was less inclined to accept the story at face value. What better way to get Shelby on Takamura's side than to feed her some unrequited love story designed to soften her up?

That, of course, had not set well with Shelby, particularly after Nathan's admonishment in the restaurant parking lot. What did he take her for, anyway? Did he really believe she was so gullible? ''You didn't see Mr. Takamura's face when he talked about Grandmother,'' she'd told Nathan hotly. ''If you had, you wouldn't be so quick to dismiss him.''

''All right,'' he'd finally acquiesced. ''I'll give him the benefit of a doubt. For now.''

But Nathan's tone warned that he was still going to keep an eye on Takamura. And on Shelby. ''Have you thought about what I said earlier?'' he'd asked her. ''About not staying alone while you're sleepwalking?''

''I've thought about it, but I haven't come to a decision.''

"At least let me drop by when I get off work," he persisted. "If you don't want me to stay, I won't."

It had been hard to argue with his reasoning, and besides, Shelby knew he was right. If her sleepwalking episodes had returned, it might not be safe for her to be alone.

The rest of the day flew by, and because her midday sojourn with Nathan had put her behind, Shelby stayed late at the shop that evening. Delfina had long since gone home when Shelby finally locked up and set the alarm. A futile effort, she reminded herself, if James had a key to the store and the code to the alarm. First thing in the morning, she'd call her grandmother and make arrangements to have both the locks and the code changed. Wouldn't hurt to have the vault combination altered as well. Where James was concerned, she couldn't be too careful.

As she neared her grandmother's house, she found herself hoping that Nathan might have arrived before her. She still had a thing about entering a darkened house alone, a fear that would abate in time, Dr. Minger had assured her. Shelby could only hope that was true.

The driveway was empty, however, when she pulled up to the house. No sign of Nathan's truck anywhere, but as Shelby got out of the car, she discovered she wasn't alone after all. Miss Scarlett came running across the yard to greet her.

The sight of the cat did wonders to lift Shelby's spirits. It was amazing how quickly she'd become accustomed to the feline's company. After little Vincent's tragic death, she wouldn't have believed it possible to become so attached to another pet, but Miss Scarlett had proven her wrong. Shelby supposed there was some truth in the old adages that time heals all wounds and life goes on.

She lifted the cat and carried her inside. Miss Scarlett leaped from Shelby's arms and went to sniff forlornly at her empty food bowl.

"No wonder you were so happy to see me," Shelby murmured, getting out the food. "It's past your dinnertime."

The phone rang as Miss Scarlett greedily attacked her bowl, and Shelby, shaking her head at the diminutive cat's voracious appetite, went to answer it. "Hello?"

"Hey, it's Nathan. Just checking to make sure it was still okay if I come by." His voice was deep and intimately low. Just the sound of it sent shivers up Shelby's backbone. Any annoyance she'd felt for him that afternoon had long since vanished.

"Sure." She moistened her lips, trying to curb her nervous excitement.

"I'll be there in a little while," he said. "Something's come up at the paper, but I shouldn't be too much longer."

"I'll see you then." She started to hang up, but he stopped her.

"Shelby?"

"Yes?"

"Uh, don't fall asleep before I get there, okay?"

She gave a shaky laugh. "I don't intend to."

After she hung up, she went upstairs to shower and change her clothes, then came back down to fix herself a light dinner. Twilight had come and gone, and the darkness outside her kitchen window deepened. Shadows moved. Leaves whispered. Night creatures began to stir.

Miss Scarlett sat huddled in the middle of the kitchen floor, warily eyeing the back door.

The skittish cat worked on Shelby's nerves. She peered out at the back porch before sitting down with her bowl of cereal.

"It's okay," she soothed Miss Scarlett. "Nathan will be here soon."

But at ten o'clock, he called again, sounding exasperated. "We've got an equipment problem in the pressroom. I can't leave yet, but I'll get there just as quickly as I can."

This time, he didn't warn her not to fall asleep, but he didn't have to. Shelby was wide-awake and restless. Her dinner finished and her bowl rinsed, she wandered through the quiet house, finally settling down on the sofa with a cozy mystery.

After a few moments of reading, she grew drowsy, but she was in no danger of falling asleep. None whatsoever. She was just a little tired....

Her eyes jerked open.

She had no idea what time it was or how long she'd been asleep. The book had fallen from her hands, and she thought for a moment the sound of the hardback hitting the floor was what had awakened her.

But it wasn't that. It wasn't a noise that had awakened her at all, but a feeling.

A sense that she wasn't alone.

Her heart thudded painfully as she lay there listening to the house.

Silence. Not even the creak of settling wood.

But the feeling persisted.

She wasn't alone.

And then Shelby realized what it was that had awakened her. What it was that caused a crawly sensation to creep up her backbone and prickle the hair at the back of her neck.

It was a smell.

Dank. Fishy.

The scent of the river.

She could smell it so clearly she might have opened all the doors and windows to the night air, but everything was closed tightly and the air conditioner hummed softly. She should not be smelling the river so strongly.

The foyer light was on. Shelby could see the stairs and the dining room beyond. Nothing stirred. Nothing crept toward her. She was safe. The smell was only her imagination. Or perhaps the wind was up, carrying the scent through the walls and windows.

But as she rose and moved quietly into the foyer, the odor became stronger. She walked into the dining room. Stronger still.

The kitchen door was closed, but the light she'd left on earlier glimmered beneath.

Shelby put a hand to the door. Her fingers trembled. Her heart pounded. It was nothing but a scent, she tried to tell herself. Nothing to be afraid of.

But it took her a moment to gather her courage, to make herself push open the kitchen door and glance inside.

Nothing seemed amiss. No signs of an intruder. Nothing out of the ordinary.

Then she noticed a dark clump lying on the linoleum near the back door—a small clod of mud. Maybe Miss Scarlett had tracked the mud into the kitchen, Shelby thought suddenly. That seemed the only logical explanation. The back door was still closed and locked. The window was shut tightly. How else could someone—or something—have gotten in while Shelby slept?

She retraced her steps into the dining room, turning on more lights. Small bits of mud were scattered about the plank flooring, but Shelby hadn't seen them before because she hadn't been looking down. She hadn't known what to look for.

She found more mud in the foyer, tiny remnants that brought on a terrible foreboding. Shelby followed the trail back into the living room, to the very sofa where she'd lain asleep only moments before.

Something had come inside and stood over her while she slept.

Chapter Fourteen

The realization hit her like a lightning bolt. Shelby gasped in fear, her breath deserting her in a painful rush.

She glanced around.

If something had been in the house only moments before she'd awakened, chances were it was still there.

In a full-blown panic, she rushed to the front door, fumbling with the lock in urgency.

Finally, the bolt slid free, and she threw open the door. A shadow moved toward her and Shelby screamed.

He grabbed her and she fought him.

"Shelby! It's me. Nathan. What's wrong? What happened?"

She struggled for a moment even after his voice penetrated her terror. Then she collapsed against him.

"Something's in...in the house," she managed to whisper.

He glanced over her shoulder, then took her hand. "Come with me."

He led her down the porch steps and across the

yard to his Bronco. Opening the door, he helped her inside. "Stay here. Keep the doors locked until I get back."

"Nathan, you can't go back in there! It might still be there…"

But he was already gone. She watched him run up the steps and disappear inside the house. Shelby glanced at the darkness surrounding the truck, and only then did she realize the significance of her words to Nathan. She'd called the intruder *it*. Not he or she or they. *It*.

A creature.

From her imagination and from her past. A thing too terrible to contemplate.

Her heart started to pound again. It was hot inside the truck, but she shivered from a bone-deep chill.

When Nathan appeared at her window, she jumped in spite of the fact that she knew immediately it was him. She released the lock, and he opened the door.

"I've checked all through the house, the upstairs, the back porch. The place is secure, Shelby." He looked a little puzzled, but not frightened. Not even overly concerned.

"But did you see anything?" she asked desperately.

He stared at her in the moonlight, his expression closed. "Like what? What frightened you so badly?"

"You didn't see the mud? How could you miss it? It was everywhere." But she'd missed it herself at first.

He ran his hands through his hair. "I didn't see anything."

Shelby slid out of the truck and started toward the

house. She was still terrified, but now her fear stemmed from something other than the intruder. Other than *it*. She couldn't allow Nathan to think she was imagining things.

Back in the house, she showed him the trail of mud from the couch back to the kitchen. It wasn't much. Not nearly as much as it had seemed earlier.

Nathan bent to examine the larger clumps in the kitchen.

"It wasn't there earlier," Shelby insisted. "You know how particular Grandmother always was about her floors. I would have noticed it. It's ingrained in me."

"I think I may have an explanation." Nathan rose. "But you aren't going to like it."

Opening the back door, he stepped onto the porch. When Shelby followed, he pointed to a pair of tennis shoes she'd left out there to dry. He picked them up and turned them over to show her the soles. Bits of mud clung to the bottoms.

Shelby stared at the shoes. "I had those on last night when I fell in the river. I put them out here to dry."

"The mud's still damp," Nathan said.

"Wait a minute." Shelby stared at him with growing suspicion. "You think I tracked in the mud last night? That it was there all day and I didn't notice it?"

"Either that, or you walked in your sleep again."

"I didn't," she said almost angrily.

"Were you awake all evening?"

Shelby swallowed. "Okay, I dozed off. But just

for a minute. I swear, Nathan, I didn't track in that mud.''

He said gently, "Are you sure? Think about it, Shelby. You could have gone out the back door and then come back in just like you did last night. The mud could have fallen off your shoes. Or even your bare feet.''

She glanced down. Her feet were wet from the dew where she'd crossed the yard to Nathan's truck. Bits of grass clung to her toes, and the bottom of her jeans were damp and stained.

She shivered violently. Was it possible? Had she left the mud?

And the scent of the river—had that been on *her*?

Nathan put his hands on her shoulders. "You're tired. Let's go back inside. You can go upstairs and get some rest.''

Shelby turned and walked numbly back into the kitchen. "I don't want to go to sleep. Could we just…talk for a while?''

Nathan nodded. "Sure. Why don't we at least sit down?''

They moved to the table.

"Would you like something to eat?'' Shelby asked him, realizing suddenly he may not have had dinner.

"No, I'm fine. But thanks.''

Another few moments ticked by. Shelby folded her hands in her lap. "Nathan? Can I ask you something?''

"Shoot.''

"What happened in Washington?''

The muscles in his jaw tensed, and she said quickly, "You don't have to tell me if you don't want to. I just thought it might, you know, take our minds off…other things.''

"It's not something I enjoy talking about, but you should probably know the truth,'' he said grimly. He got up and walked to the window to stare out. After a moment, he turned back to her, leaning against the counter. "It happened about three years ago. I'd had a lot of success early on as a reporter, first in Memphis and then in Washington. I was something of a rebel, I guess. Arrogant. Hardheaded. Too full of my own self-importance. So sure I was going to be the next Woodward or Bernstein.''

That didn't sound like the man Shelby knew. Ambitious, probably. Hardheaded, definitely. But not arrogant. Not self-important. In spite of his penchant for adventure, Nathan had always had his feet planted firmly on the ground. Shelby wondered what had made him stray so far off course.

He frowned briefly, as if reading her mind. "I got wind of a possible scandal involving a congressman. Just the type of story I could sink my teeth into. The guy was young, ambitious, a rising star for his party. And according to my source, he was in the pocket of several large corporations in his district that had been heavily fined over the past several years for EPA violations. My source claimed to be one of the congressman's top aides. He knew where all the bodies were buried, he said. He started feeding me information on how the congressman would vote on key pieces of environmental legislation, and he was right on the money every time. I figured at the very least the congressman was being lobbied hard by the corporations back in his district. So I started an investigation. The story began to develop hard. There were other reporters on the trail, and I didn't want to be scooped. So on the eve of a House vote on a major environmental bill, I went with what I had, citing the congressman's past voting record and 'a close source' that tied him to the corporations.''

"What happened?''

Nathan glanced away. "What my source didn't tell me was that he had an ax to grind with his boss. He didn't like the congressman's record on environmental issues, so he made up the bribery charges in order to ruin the man's reputation. It all came out, of course, but not before the damage was done. When the story first broke, the congressman's wife had a nervous breakdown.''

Shelby didn't know what to say. "This doesn't sound like you, Nathan.''

He winced. "I have a hard time believing it myself sometimes, but the congressman wasn't the only one with ambitions. The news business is cutthroat, Shelby. Ruthless and competitive. I'm not making excuses. I guess I'm just trying to explain how I became…seduced by visions of my own grandeur.'' He paused. "You know the really ironic part of all this? After the congressman was defeated, other charges against him surfaced. He actually *was* taking illegal money from corporations in his district to vote against environmental legislation. But the fact that he was guilty didn't let me off the hook. What I did was wrong, and my reputation was ruined. I left town without a shred of credibility. No reputable paper would touch me after that.''

Shelby got up and went to stand beside him. "So that's why you came back here?"

His gaze met hers. Something flickered in those dark depths. Regret. Guilt. Shame. She knew some of what he was feeling, and it made her want to reach out to him even more. He'd made mistakes. He was human. Somehow Shelby found that a bit reassuring.

"This is my last chance," he said. "I guess that's why I've been looking for a valid story. Something important. I want another shot at covering something worthy, without compromising my journalistic integrity."

"But you've already done that," Shelby said. "You've already written a worthy story. Don't you remember how touched Gayla Weathers was by the article you wrote about Danny? She wanted to have it framed so her kids could remember their father the way you did. What could be more important than bringing solace to a family in so much pain? You *have* done something important, Nathan, and you should be very proud."

He gazed at her for a moment, lifting his hand to her face. "Why is it you could always make me feel better about myself than I deserve to?"

"Why is it you've always been so hard on yourself? We all make mistakes, and you've paid for yours."

"That still doesn't wipe the slate clean."

"Maybe not. But maybe everything happens for a reason. Your mistakes eventually brought you back here, and now you have the chance to do good work in this town. You have the opportunity to touch more lives than you might ever have in Washington. You see that, don't you?''

''Maybe I'm beginning to.'' He closed the distance between them, putting his other hand to her face. ''Why is it that I want to kiss you so badly at this moment?'' he murmured.

Shelby's heart gave an erratic thud against her chest. ''What's stopping you?''

He stared down at her for a moment, as if she'd caught him completely by surprise. Then he lowered his head and brushed his lips against hers. It was a light, teasing kiss, but Shelby knew that Nathan was deadly serious.

So was she. She parted her lips, kissing him back, and for a moment, her response seemed to stun him. He drew back, staring down at her again, searching her face. His expression was intense, his gaze dark and smoldering. Then he wrapped his arms around her, lifting her, and crushed her mouth with his.

A million sensations flooded through Shelby. A million thoughts. She shouldn't be doing this. It was all wrong.

Oh, but it felt so right!

She shouldn't be kissing another man. But this wasn't just another man.

This was Nathan!

This wasn't the time or the place. She could get hurt.

And yet...

What time would be better? A year from now? Two years? Thirty? How long before she would feel free enough to love another man? How long before she felt safe enough to risk her heart again?

There were no guarantees in life. No one knew that better than Shelby. But maybe the risk was what made life worth living.

And she did want Nathan.

More than she could ever have imagined.

She wanted his arms around her. His mouth on hers. She wanted him to kiss her over and over until nothing of her fear remained. Until the only thing that mattered was the slow, sweet desire burning its way through her.

And then she wanted more.

Her heart was pounding so hard it was almost painful. Her breath came quick and hot. When they finally broke apart, Nathan let her slip back to the floor, and Shelby swayed for a moment, clinging to him.

"Did that meet your expectations?" he asked, in a voice that was like dark satin. Unbearably sensuous. Undeniably sexy.

Meet her expectations? Shelby thought, her senses reeling.

Nathan's kiss had far exceeded her wildest dreams.

NATHAN STOOD OVER Shelby's bed, watching her sleep. He'd rushed up the stairs a few minutes earlier when he'd heard her cry out, but she was safe and sound in her bed. In the throes of a nightmare, he suspected.

She was quiet now, her breathing even, her expression untroubled. She smiled a little in her sleep, and Nathan turned to leave.

"Don't go," she whispered.

He moved back to the bed. "I thought you were asleep."

"I was, but a dream woke me up. How long have you been standing there?" She cuddled her pillow to her chest, gazing up at him. She didn't seem annoyed, but maybe it would have been better if she had. As it was, she looked a little too tempting, lying there in the moonlight, all soft and rumpled from sleep.

"You cried out in your sleep," he said. "I came up to check on you."

"Did I?" She frowned. "I don't remember."

"I'd better get out of here and let you get back to sleep."

"Nathan." She sat up in bed, hugging her knees. Her silky pajamas shimmered in the moonlight. The fabric looked soft and inviting. Begging for his touch. "Could we talk about what happened earlier?" she said.

"You mean the mud you found in the house?" He sat down on the edge of the bed.

She shook her head. Her gaze met his. "I mean the kiss."

His heart gave a hard thud against the wall of his chest, but he was careful not to react outwardly. "What about it?"

"You asked if it had met my expectations. I didn't answer you. But it did. It was…incredible."

The message in her eyes was unmistakable, but Nathan didn't dare let himself hope. Didn't dare let himself move too fast. He took her hand. "What are you saying, Shelby?"

"That I want you to kiss me again." Her voice was hardly more than a whisper.

"Shelby—"

"It's okay." He was still uncertain, but she sounded very sure of herself. She drew their linked hands up to her cheek. "I trust you, Nathan. I always have."

Her words took his breath away. He lay down beside her on the bed, and they rolled to face one another. "Are you sure about all this?"

She nodded, her eyes a deep, misty blue in the moonlight. "Aren't you?"

He gave a low laugh. "Not exactly. But that's never stopped me before, has it?"

She smiled and lifted her hand to his face. He closed his eyes at the gentleness. At the dream that seemed on the verge of finally coming true.

He'd loved Shelby for so long.

No other woman had ever come close to taking her place in his heart. That was why it had been so easy to focus on his career, to let his ambition rule him. But now here she was, in his arms at last…

He touched her hair, letting his fingers slip through the short, silky strands, marveling at the softness, the radiance in the moonlight.

He touched her face, tracing the outline of her jaw, the soft, full texture of her lips.

He touched her throat, lingering on the ridge of a scar, knowing instinctively what had caused it. For a moment, a terrible rage clouded his passion. He wanted to kill Albert Lunt. With his bare hands.

But Shelby seemed to know what he was thinking,

and she put her hand over his. "It's okay," she whispered again.

No, it wasn't okay. It would never be okay that Shelby had been hurt, threatened in any way. It wasn't okay that Nathan hadn't been there to protect her. But he was here now, and there wasn't anything in the world he wouldn't do for her.

He kissed her then, and her lips parted for him. Her tongue met his without hesitation, and she wrapped her arms around him, pressing her body to his. He'd never known what a truly sexual being Shelby was until that moment. She'd always seemed so innocent to him. So above earthly needs. But her hands on him were greedy, her body against his demanding. She was a fantasy come to life and then some.

He slid off her pajamas. Only then did she seem a little hesitant, but she made no move to cover herself. She lay on top of the sheets, letting the moonlight—and Nathan's eyes—adore her.

And he thought to himself that he had never seen anything so beautiful.

He touched her as if she were made of fine porcelain, and Shelby was moved by his tenderness. But she didn't want to be touched like porcelain. She wanted to be touched like a woman. She wanted him demanding. Greedy. The way she felt.

But it wouldn't do to rush it. It had been so long since she'd...

No! She wouldn't think about that. Tonight was for Nathan. Only Nathan.

She guided his hand to where she wanted it to be, and his response was quick, surprised, delighted. He stroked her, whispered to her, made her burn for him and then she did the same to him.

After a long while, he rose over her, gazed down at her, and Shelby's heart almost stopped.

It was heaven, being with Nathan. Like nothing she'd ever experienced before. He knew exactly where to touch her, exactly when to hold her, as if he could intuit her every need. His kisses were deep and shattering, his caresses hot and urgent. Their movements became almost frenzied as the need began to build, that glowing, desperate hunger…

Shelby clung to him, cried out for him….

And then it happened, that moment of complete ecstasy, that shuddering crescendo of emotions and sensations, followed by an almost devastating vulnerability.

She tried to turn away from Nathan, but he wouldn't let her. He kissed her face all over, brushing his lips lightly against her forehead, her cheeks, her mouth.

And then he held her for a long time until she finally fell asleep.

NATHAN CAME abruptly awake with a certainty that something was wrong. Shelby had fallen asleep wrapped in his arms, but she was gone now. The knowledge that she had slipped away from him so easily jolted him. He sat up in bed, reaching for his clothes, then paused.

She was standing at the window, naked. Moonlight silvered the perfect contours of her body, and desire shot through him again. He got out of bed and went to her.

"Shelby?"

She didn't answer him, didn't turn when he touched her lightly on the arm. Her gaze seemed fixed on something distant. He glanced out the window, saw nothing but moonlight on water. Shadows moving gently in a breeze.

"Shelby? Come on back to bed, honey."

This time she turned at the sound of his voice, but he didn't think she'd heard him. Her eyes were glazed, vacant. She was sound asleep.

She reached her hand to touch his cheek. "Michael?"

Chapter Fifteen

Nathan was gone the next morning when Shelby awakened. She felt a keen sense of disappointment as she stared at his pillow. But then she remembered that he had to be at the paper early. And it was late. She'd slept right through the alarm.

Jumping out of bed, she showered and dressed for work so quickly, she hardly had time to think about last night. About what had happened. About the guilt that was already starting to eat away at her.

But throughout the morning, no matter how busy she kept herself, her mind would wander and without warning, she would be back in Nathan's arms. Reliving every moment of their lovemaking.

And then the guilt would inevitably follow, even though she told herself over and over she had nothing to feel guilty about. She'd been a loving and faithful wife to her husband. If she and Michael had lived together to a ripe old age, her loyalty would never have wavered. She would never, ever have betrayed him.

But even so...

It had happened so quickly with Nathan, and it wasn't like Shelby to be so impulsive. So reckless.

And yet Nathan had always brought out a side of her that no one else could. He'd always made her believe in herself in a way no one else ever had.

AND SO IT WAS OVER. Before it had barely started.

Nathan stared out the window of his uncle's office, tuning out Virgil's suggestion for the lead article of that evening's edition. All he could think about was Shelby standing at that window, asleep, reaching for her dead husband.

In that moment, everything had become crystal clear for Nathan. He'd been living in a fantasy world, clinging to a dream that was never meant to be. Shelby didn't love him. She couldn't, because she was still in love with Michael.

Nathan had been a substitute, nothing more. A way to assuage her loneliness. For a while.

"Did you hear what I said?"

He turned to his uncle. "Do what you want."

Virgil looked completely taken aback. "What?"

"Look, I've got something I need to take care of. Can you hold down the fort without me?"

"I've been holding it down for thirty years without you," Virgil grumbled. Then he glanced at Nathan worriedly. "You want to tell me what's eating you this morning?"

Nathan didn't want to confide in anyone about his feelings for Shelby, especially his uncle. Virgil was the last person who could ever understand. He had never married. As far as Nathan knew, he'd never had even one serious relationship, although there had been women.

Nathan had worked at the paper all through high school, and he could still remember the late-night visits of various females to the paper, his uncle's closed office door. And then when the women left—and for a long time afterward—his uncle would have a hard time looking Nathan in the face, as if he felt tremendous guilt for some reason, as if he'd been caught in the act of betrayal.

The memory made Nathan think unaccountably of Yoshi Takamura's claim that he'd loved Shelby's grandmother for thirty years. That he'd waited for her all this time. Was there someone like that in Virgil's life? Was that why he'd never married?

It didn't matter. Nathan still didn't want to unload his troubles. "I don't want to talk about it," he said.

"Didn't think so." Virgil sighed. "All right, son. You go do what you have to do. Take as much time as you need. I'll take care of things here."

"Thanks."

"Nathan?"

He turned at the door and glanced back.

"This have anything to do with Shelby Westmoreland?"

"Her name is August," Nathan said grimly, "But why do you ask?"

Virgil's gaze on him sharpened. "Because you haven't been the same since she came back to town. You've got it bad for her, don't you?"

Nathan shrugged. "I'll get over it."

"Don't count on it, son."

THE BELLS over the shop door tinkled, and Shelby glanced up, almost expecting to see her uncle James or his lawyer or both of them. She hadn't heard from James in a day or two, but Shelby didn't fool herself into thinking that he'd given up on his plan. If he had incurred gambling debts, as Nathan's information seemed to suggest, then he could be a very desperate man.

But instead of James, Nathan walked through the door. Shelby's face flushed red-hot, seeing him. A thousand memories came back to her. The feel of his lips against her throat. The whisper of his fingers down her thigh.

Was he thinking about it, too?

A tentative smile touched her lips, but then faded the moment she saw his eyes—not warm, as she would have imagined, but cold and distant. "Is... something wrong?"

"Could we go into the office? We need to talk." His clipped tones were as ominous as his eyes.

What on earth had happened since this morning? Was he regretting the night they'd spent together? Having second thoughts about *her?*

He closed the door and then walked over to the widow to stare out, as if he couldn't quite meet her gaze. Shelby's hand went to the scarf at her throat, an action that was automatic when she felt threatened.

"I think it might be a good idea if we slow things down for a while."

His words were like a slap in the face, but Shelby had too much pride to let him see how badly he'd hurt her. "If that's how you feel, fine."

He shrugged, not looking at her. "I still don't

think you should be staying alone. Maybe there's someone else who could...?''

"No," she said coolly. "I don't need anyone to stay with me. I'll be fine."

"What if you sleepwalk all the way down to the river?" he said, turning at last to face her.

"That isn't your concern, is it?" Shelby gazed at him a moment, unable to believe how quickly things had changed between them. How fast it had all come to an end. Last night might only have been a dream, except...it wasn't. Their time together had meant everything to her. A step forward. A new beginning.

And now it was over. Just like that.

She didn't understand it. "Tell me something, Nathan. What's this all about?"

"I just think we're moving a little too fast—"

"You came to me," she cut in angrily. "You were the one who wanted to be friends. You're the one who wanted me to help you with the Takamura story. You're the one who pursued *me*. Was it all just a lie? A way to get me into bed?"

Pain flashed in his eyes. "No. That wasn't my intent. It just...happened."

Heat flooded her face. "That's all you can say about it? It just...*happened*?" Tears smarted behind Shelby's lids, but she blinked them away. She wouldn't give him the satisfaction. "So let me guess," she said. "If you weren't trying to get me into bed, then you must have been after a story. When will it run? Tonight? It'll be an updated version, I imagine. One that includes the tracks I saw on my front porch and the mud I found in the house.

How convenient that you were there. And how James will love reading about it.''

Nathan's gaze narrowed on her. A muscle throbbed in his cheek. ''What are you accusing me of, Shelby?''

''We both know how far you're willing to go to get the kind of story you want.'' The moment she said the words, Shelby regretted them, but it was too late to take them back.

His gaze turned icy cold. ''That was a low blow.''

She lifted her chin, refusing to back down. ''Just tell me the truth. Did you use me to get a story?''

He stared at her for a moment, as if she were a stranger. ''I never used you. Not once. But it's a pity you can't say the same thing.''

She said in shock, ''What are you talking about? I never used you.''

''Really? What about last night?'' Nathan walked over to stand in front of her. He took her arms, gazing down into her eyes. ''Who were you thinking about last night when we made love? Whose face did you see over you? Whose lips and hands were on you?''

She felt the color drain from her face at his insinuation.

''I was a substitute, wasn't I?'' he demanded. ''It wasn't me you were with at all.''

''No! That's not true—''

He dropped his hands from her arms and stepped back. ''Then why did you call me Michael?''

BY THE TIME Shelby got home that evening, the weight of the world seemed to rest on her shoulders.

Her emotions ran the gamut. She was hurt, bewildered, tired, angry, sad. So very sad. She felt as if she'd just lost her best friend—and she had.

She *couldn't* have mistaken Nathan for Michael. Why would she have? There'd been no doubt in her mind who she was with. No doubt that anyone had ever made her feel the way Nathan had.

So why would he accuse her of using him? Was it simply a way out for him?

Weary and heartsick, Shelby parked in the drive and got out of her grandmother's car. There was still daylight, but the sun had set. She could smell the river, and it reminded her of the scent in the house last night. Or had it all been her imagination? Shelby didn't seem to be sure of anything anymore.

She crossed the yard and had started up the porch steps when she heard a cat crying nearby. She hesitated on the bottom stair, glancing around. "Miss Scarlett? Here kitty, kitty, kitty."

The meow came again, loud, close. Demanding.

Shelby hoped the cat hadn't gotten herself stuck up a tree again. She wasn't certain she had enough energy to mount a rescue tonight.

"Miss Scarlett?"

Then Shelby saw her. Amber eyes glowed between the lattice slats underneath the house.

Backing down the steps, Shelby walked hesitantly over to the house and knelt. The cat stuck one little paw through the slats, like a convict being visited in prison.

Shelby reached a finger inside and rubbed the cat's head. "What's the matter? Can't you find your way out?"

The openings between the slats were too small even for Miss Scarlett's petite figure. But she'd found a way in, so there had to be a way out.

Walking around the house, Shelby searched the lattice for missing slats. All the while, she called to Miss Scarlett, and the cat's plaintive cries answered her.

Shelby was around the back of the house now. She hadn't seen an opening, and the gate was closed. She had no idea how the cat had gotten herself penned inside.

Moving to the gate, Shelby started to swing it open, but then she hesitated, remembering the sounds she'd heard the other night and the fish scales and the mud she'd found on the gate the next morning.

A dark dread descended over her. She didn't want to open that gate, but she had to. She had to free Miss Scarlett. But Shelby had a terrible feeling that something besides her grandmother's cat lurked in the shadows.

She drew the gate open quickly. A black blur streaked by her. Miss Scarlett. She turned to call to the cat when a shadow moved from within. Shelby's heart bolted to her throat, but before she could back away from the opening, a hand—inhuman it seemed to her—reached out and pulled her into the shadows.

Shelby tried to scream, tried to fight. But that first moment of shock cost her dearly. Something hit her on the back of the head, and her skull exploded in pain.

THE LIGHT FADED QUICKLY, and Nathan was getting more uneasy by the minute. There'd been no answer at either the shop or the house when he'd tried to call Shelby. She should have been home by now. He'd even called the hospital to see if she'd gone to see her grandmother. But Miss Annabel hadn't heard from her, either, and all Nathan had succeeded in doing was worrying the poor woman.

He'd finally managed to reassure her that Shelby was fine, but Nathan wasn't so certain. In spite of what he'd told Shelby earlier, he could no more leave her alone tonight than he could forget all the years that he'd loved her. She was still Shelby, and every instinct he possessed was telling him that she might be in trouble. Maybe not this minute. Maybe not even tonight. But the sleepwalking episodes could very well be symptomatic of a deeper problem. The imagined footprints and the mud—

Wait a minute. *He'd* seen the mud. She hadn't imagined that. He'd assumed that it had either been there earlier and she hadn't noticed it, or she'd walked outside in her sleep.

But what if something really had come up her front steps? Been in her house last night? Something other than Shelby's imagination. Was it possible someone was deliberately trying to frighten her? Make her think she was seeing things?

Nathan was more convinced than ever that Shelby's uncle was behind the missing pearls. He'd even had the gall to try and secure a loan using them as collateral. If he had that much nerve, if he was that desperate, what else might he be willing to pull?

If he really intended to press for a competency hearing to try and wrest control of Miss Annabel's finances from her, then his first move would be to get Shelby out of the way. Not only would she fight for her grandmother, but there was also a very good chance that even if the judge ruled Miss Annabel incompetent, Shelby might be appointed the guardian. With Shelby gone, there would be no one left but James.

Nathan's mouth tightened as he turned onto the river road, heading for Shelby's place. There was another explanation, one that seemed too implausible to even consider. And yet Nathan had never quite been able to dismiss it.

What if Shelby's monster was real?

"Idiot," he muttered, scowling at the road.

He was approaching Danny Weathers's secret spot. Shelby's place was another mile or so up the road. Even though there was still some light, Nathan could barely see the water through the trees. But as he drove by, his headlights glinted off something metal. It was only an impression as he sped by, but he could have sworn there was a car pulled off the road and camouflaged in a deep thicket. In all likelihood, Nathan would never have seen the vehicle if he hadn't known about Danny's spot, if he hadn't been looking off at the water.

Someone was there, in the secret spot. And that someone had taken great trouble to conceal his vehicle.

For a moment, Nathan was torn. He had an urgent need to keep going. Maybe Shelby was home by now. Maybe they could have a long talk. Straighten out a few things. He could apologize for being such a jerk earlier. Shelby couldn't help it that she still loved her husband. She wasn't the kind of person who could turn her feelings off and on. She would remain loyal to him, even in death. That was what made her Shelby.

Still…

Nathan threw on the brakes and reversed the Bronco down the road, slowing when he got to Danny's spot. Pulling off the road, he got out of his truck and walked over to the hidden car. It was a late-model sedan, and for a moment, he just stared at it.

Then a terrible dread washed over him.

He knew that car. He'd seen it only hours before.

SHELBY CAME TO slowly. For a moment, she thought she was trapped underneath her grandmother's house, but then she realized she could see stars. A breeze drifted over her. She was outside somewhere.

She turned her head, but before she had more than a glance at her surroundings, strong hands grabbed her from behind and hauled her up. Shelby tried to struggle, tried to see who—what—had her, but suddenly they were tumbling backward. Icy water splashed over her, and Shelby barely had time to take a deep breath before her head was plunged beneath the river.

Panic exploded inside her. She lashed out with her hands. Kicked with her feet. Something dark and terrible had her and was pulling her deeper and deeper into the water.

Down, down, they descended. To the muddy river bottom.

Shelby's lungs screamed in protest. She fought, but she couldn't get free.

She was drowning! *Dear God, help me!*

Suddenly there was a light. A thin beam cutting a fissure through the thick water. The light picked out a large shadow on the bottom, and Shelby was dragged toward it.

Something touched her leg.

She jerked. Fought. Reached out with her hands.

Metal. Nathan's haunted car.

Her captor grabbed her around the throat with one arm. The light was wedged against the bumper. For several precious seconds, he…it struggled with the trunk.

Bubbles shot out as the lid opened, and then Shelby was thrust toward it. She grabbed frantically at the car to keep the trunk from closing over her. Something came loose in her hand. She clutched it like a lifeline, and then, as the light arced again toward the car, she knew that her time had come.

A skeletal hand beckoned to her.

NATHAN SAW a boat in the water, and he dove in and swam toward it. A line had been tied to an oar lock and ran beneath the surface of the water. Taking a deep breath, he grabbed the rope and followed it down.

Without a light, he was swimming blindly. He kept the line between his hands, and it led him straight to the bottom.

To Shelby.

He would never have seen them if not for the light. Glowing dimly in the murky water, it was Nathan's only guide. Swimming hard, he rammed into his uncle, knocking him way from Shelby.

Nathan sensed more than saw her float away from the car.

He tried to get to her, but Virgil grabbed him. He was old, but he still had the advantage. He had air, and Nathan didn't.

Grabbing for the regulator, Nathan tried to even the odds.

SHELBY WAS TOO WEAK to fight her way to the surface. Beyond pain and panic now, she slipped into a dangerous lethargy.

Then something bumped hard against her, sending her several feet toward the surface.

Another bump, and Shelby's head broke the water. She drew air deeply into her lungs, coughing, sputtering, still deeply panicked.

Somehow, she would never know how, she managed to pull herself over the side of the boat and collapse in the bottom.

VIRGIL FOUGHT HIM HARD. In spite of his age, he was still a strong man, and Nathan was out of air. His lungs were screaming. He had to get to the surface. He had to breathe.

But Virgil was also a badly frightened man. A man fighting for his life. He swung at Nathan with the light, but it slipped from his hand and floated to the bottom. The silt was thick from their struggles, but the light cut an eerie path through the muck. Nathan saw something on the bottom that made his blood go cold.

Eyes gleaming.

A mouth gaping.

As Virgil reached down for the light, the logger-head's powerful jaws snapped closed over his hand.

Nathan burst up out of the water, sucking air deeply into his lungs. He glanced around wildly for Shelby, and then he saw her in the boat. She was leaning over the side, peering down into the water.

She appeared to be safe, but Nathan watched her for a moment to make certain. He knew he would have to go down again. No matter what his uncle had done, he couldn't leave him to that fate.

But, as he readied himself to dive, Nathan spotted a series of bubbles several yards away. They were heading for the bank, as if someone was swimming just beneath the surface of the water.

Somehow Virgil had managed to free himself, and now he was trying to get away. Nathan was too weary to care.

He swam toward Shelby.

When he pulled himself over the side of the boat, she fell into his arms. "You're safe," she kept saying over and over. "Oh, thank God."

He held her tightly, the realization of how close he'd come to losing her for good hitting him hard. "It was my uncle Virgil," he finally told her. "He tried to kill you."

Shelby pulled back and stared at him in shock. "But why? I hardly know him."

Nathan shrugged. "I have no idea, but you can be damn sure I'm going to find out."

Nathan didn't want to release Shelby. He couldn't get enough of touching her. He drew her back into his arms, and just when he thought their emotions were quieting somewhat, Shelby gasped, pulling away from him. "Someone's over there." She nodded toward the bank.

Nathan turned, expecting to see his uncle heading back into the water toward them, but instead, the figure rose from the bank and walked gracefully into the woods. "It's a woman."

"Delfina," Shelby whispered. "I wonder—"

"What?"

She glanced up at him. In the fading twilight, her eyes gleamed with awe. "When I was under water, I didn't think I was going to make it to the surface. I'd almost given up, but something pushed me upward. I wonder if it could have been Delfina."

"It's possible. After tonight, I guess I could believe just about anything," he said ironically.

Shelby was staring down at her hand. Something lay in her palm.

"What's that?"

She held it out to him. "It came loose from the car while I was struggling to get away. I think it's a necklace. Or at least, what's left of one. It must have gotten hung on the trunk lid."

Nathan stared at the pendant in Shelby's hand. The center pearl had long since disintegrated, and the gold filigree was encrusted with mud. But he could see the sparkle of tiny diamonds in the moonlight.

"Nathan? Is something wrong?"

He lifted his gaze to Shelby's. "That was my mother's necklace."

THEY WERE back at the house, clean, dry and safe, and awaiting word from the sheriff. He came knocking on Shelby's door just before midnight. She led him into the kitchen and poured him a cup of coffee.

"We found Virgil," he said grimly. "He was trying to make a run for it, just like you said he would. Once he saw us, he just plumb gave up and sobbed like a baby. We took him in, and he broke down and told us everything. It's been eatin' away at him for years. I think it was a relief to get it off his chest."

Between sips of coffee, Sheriff McCaid related the story to Nathan and Shelby—how Virgil had been in love with Nathan's mother. How he'd tried for years to get her to run off with him. How they'd struggled at the paper late one night when she'd finally said, out of desperation, that she was going to tell Caleb. She'd fallen and struck her head, and the blow had killed her instantly.

"Virgil swears it was an accident. I guess we'll have to let a jury decide that," McCaid said.

Terrified by what had happened, Virgil panicked. He hid Katherine's body, then wrote a note, forging her handwriting and saying that she'd left town with another man. He knew his brother would believe it because Caleb, his insecurities fed by Virgil, had never felt he deserved a woman like Katherine. Had never thought he could give her the kind of life she deserved.

Both brothers had been raised in poverty, but Caleb wasn't a scholar like Virgil, nor had he had his brother's ambition. He hadn't been able to rise above their humble beginnings, and Virgil had never let him forget.

The note worked, of course, because the only two people who saw it would never think to challenge it.

Nathan was only ten years old and Caleb couldn't read.

Virgil waited until the next night, and then took the body underwater, to an old car he'd seen once while diving with his brother. Prying open the trunk, he stuffed Katherine's body inside, then wired shut the lid.

"You saw him coming up out of the river that night, Shelby. He was in an old diving suit he'd made for himself. He must have looked a sight, especially in the dead of night like that. Virgil was your monster."

"But that car is over a mile away from here," Shelby said.

"Virgil was badly panicked. He got turned around underwater. The currents carried him downstream. That's why he made sure he had a lead rope this time so he could pull himself back up to his boat. You can imagine the emotional state he was in when he came up out of the water that night. Then he saw you and I guess he went a little crazy. He came after you, but you made it to the house before he could get to you."

"And then he wrote all those stories about me," Shelby said. "Wasn't he afraid I'd eventually realize what I'd seen?"

"That's exactly why he wrote them. You claimed you saw a monster. Who was going to believe anything you said after that?"

"And he's been terrorizing her ever since she came back to town," Nathan said quietly.

McCaid nodded. "He's kept tabs on you all these years, Shelby. When he heard you were coming back, he thought he could scare you off at first. He even found out where Miss Annabel kept a spare key to this house from Aline Henley, so he could come and go as he pleased. But then he realized that you two…well, that you were getting close. He was afraid you'd never leave, and that being out here on the river, you'd eventually remember. When Danny Weathers started messing around near that car, he got really desperate. He says Danny's death was an accident, too, but that's a little hard to swallow, considering. When you decided to investigate Danny's death, Nathan, it all snowballed on him.''

''I always thought he was a good guy,'' Nathan said. ''He was a role model for me. But all these years, he's let me think my mother left me. He must have written those Christmas and birthday cards himself, and had someone out of town send them to me. And then the one time my mother supposedly called, Virgil was the one who answered the phone. No one else talked to her. He let my dad die, thinking she betrayed him. You did see a monster that night after all, Shelby.''

She reached over and took his hand.

Sheriff McCaid cleared his throat and stood. ''I better let you folks get some rest. I'll need to get statements from both of you, but that can wait till morning.''

Shelby and Nathan walked him out. After his car had disappeared down the road, she turned to Nathan. ''I'm so sorry about all this.''

''You're sorry. He's my uncle. When I think about the hell he put you through back then. What he's tried to do to you since you came back.'' Nathan's

expression was colder than Shelby had ever seen it. "I wouldn't blame you if you couldn't stand the thought of being near me."

"But none of this is your fault."

"Maybe not. But I'm feeling pretty guilty tonight. Not just about Virgil, but for the way I attacked you this afternoon. I don't know what came over me, Shelby."

"I think I do." She gazed up at him in the moonlight. "There's something I need to tell you."

He seemed to brace himself. "Yes?"

"I knew exactly who I was with last night, Nathan. I knew who was kissing me, holding me. Loving me. I knew, because I'd never felt that way before in my life."

His gaze deepened. "You mean that?"

"With all my heart. I love you, Nathan."

"You don't know how long I've waited to hear you say that," he said softly. "I love you, too. From the moment I first laid eyes on you."

He bent and kissed her then. And for a long moment, the world around them faded. They didn't notice how the moonlight glinted silver on the river. How the breeze whispered through the trees. How the clock inside struck midnight.

They didn't hear the splash in the water, or the large circles that undulated against the bank.

Epilogue

A year later...

It was a perfect day for a wedding.

The sun shone like priceless jewels through the stained-glass window of the church, and the scent of roses filled the air. Expectant eyes turned as the wedding march sounded.

Shelby's hands trembled as she clutched her bouquet. Her gaze lifted, and at the end of the aisle, she saw Nathan, smiling, handsome in his tuxedo.

Looking radiant in a lilac dress, her grandmother clutched his arm. She was almost recovered now, but she still walked with a cane and probably always would. It wasn't going to slow her down any, she'd declared. Not one bit.

But in spite of her assertion, she'd recently retired and Shelby was now running the shop, with Delfina's help. The girl was still a little strange at times, but her abject devotion to Annabel had endeared her to Shelby, even though she still wondered sometimes about the night she'd seen Delfina sitting on the bank, casting pebbles into the water. And the night

Shelby had almost drowned, when someone—or something—had pushed her toward the surface. Shelby had never asked Delfina about either of those events, because she'd come to the conclusion that some things were best left in the shadowy realm of the unknown.

Nathan was now publisher and editor of the *Argus*. His uncle, bitterly remorseful and guilt-ridden, had died in prison three months ago, leaving the paper free and clear to Nathan.

Shelby's uncle James had left town when confronted about the pearls missing from the Pearl Cove's vault. Shelby knew Yoshi Takamura had convinced James to return the stolen pearls, then Yoshi had hired him and sent him off on some foreign excursion so that he couldn't cause further harm to Annabel's peace of mind. For that, Shelby would be eternally grateful.

She glanced over and smiled shyly at Yoshi, but his gaze was on her grandmother. On the woman he'd loved for thirty years. On the woman who was about to become his wife.

How much all their lives had changed in just one short year, Shelby reflected.

Beneath the delicate petals in her bouquet, she glimpsed the twinkle of diamonds surrounding a fragile silvery-blue pearl ring, the exact shade of her dress. The pearl, as beautiful as it was rare, was one Nathan had been saving for her for a very long time, he'd confided. The color had always reminded him of her eyes.

Around her throat, she wore his mother's restored pendant. She touched the creamy center pearl and glanced up, her eyes brimming. Somewhere, some-how, Shelby wanted to believe that Caleb Dallas knew the truth about his wife. That the two of them were together again, now that Katherine had been released from her watery tomb.

The tragedy made Shelby all the more grateful that she'd found Nathan again, after all these years and that she had been given this second chance at hap-piness. She intended to make the most of it. Starting this very moment. And if Caleb and Katherine were looking down from heaven and smiling, so was Mi-chael. Shelby believed that with all her heart.

As Nathan and her grandmother approached the altar, he gently placed Annabel's hand inside Yoshi's. Then moving to Shelby's side, he took her hand and lifted it to his lips.

It was a perfect day for a double wedding.

INDULGE IN A QUIET MOMENT
WITH HARLEQUIN

Get a FREE

Quiet Moments Bath Spa

with just two proofs of purchase from any of our four special collector's editions in May.

Harlequin® is sure to make your time special this Mother's Day with four special collector's editions featuring a short story *PLUS* a complete novel packaged together in one volume!

Collection #1 Intrigue abounds in a collection featuring *New York Times* bestselling author Barbara Delinsky and Kelsey Roberts.

Collection #2 Relationships? Weddings? Children? = *New York Times* bestselling author Debbie Macomber and Tara Taylor Quinn at their best!

Collection #3 Escape to the past with *New York Times* bestselling author Heather Graham and Gayle Wilson.

Collection #4 Go West! With *New York Times* bestselling author Joan Johnston and Vicki Lewis Thompson!

Plus Special Consumer Campaign!

Each of these four collector's editions will feature a
"FREE QUIET MOMENTS BATH SPA" offer.
See inside book in May for details.

Only from
◆ HARLEQUIN®
Makes any time special ®

Don't miss out! Look for this exciting promotion on sale in May 2001, at your favorite retail outlet.

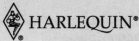

Harlequin invites you to walk down the aisle . . .

To honor our year long celebration of weddings, we are offering an exciting opportunity for you to own the Harlequin Bride Doll. Handcrafted in fine bisque porcelain, the wedding doll is dressed for her wedding day in a cream satin gown accented by lace trim. She carries an exquisite traditional bridal bouquet and wears a cathedral-length dotted Swiss veil. Embroidered flowers cascade down her lace overskirt to the scalloped hemline; underneath all is a multi-layered crinoline.

Join us in our celebration of weddings by sending away for your own Harlequin Bride Doll. This doll regularly retails for $74.95 U.S./approx. $108.68 CDN. One doll per household. Requests must be received no later than June 30, 2001. Offer good while quantities of gifts last. Please allow 6-8 weeks for delivery. Offer good in the U.S. and Canada only. Become part of this exciting offer!

Simply complete the order form and mail to:
"A Walk Down the Aisle"

IN U.S.A
P.O. Box 9057
3010 Walden Ave.
Buffalo, NY 14240-9057

IN CANADA
P.O. Box 622
Fort Erie, Ontario
L2A 5X3

Enclosed are eight (8) proofs of purchase found on the last page of every specially marked Harlequin series book and $3.75 check or money order (for postage and handling). Please send my Harlequin Bride Doll to:

_____

Name (PLEASE PRINT)

_____

Address   Apt. #

_____

City   State/Prov.   Zip/Postal Code

_____

Account # (if applicable)   098 KIK DAEW

HARLEQUIN®
Makes any time special®

Visit us at www.eHarlequin.com

┌ ─ ─ ─ ─ ─ ─ ─ ─ ─ ─ ─ ─ ─ ─ ┐
A Walk Down the Aisle
Free Bride Doll Offer
One Proof-of-Purchase
└ ─ ─ ─ ─ ─ ─ ─ ─ ─ ─ ─ ─ ─ ─ ┘

PHWDAPOP